IN THE NOW

JENNIFER ANN SHORE

D1377334

Digital ISBN: 978-1-7326083-8-2

Print ISBN: 978-1-7326083-9-9

Cover Image: Munmun Singh

*For Reno—for all the
trouble we got into and
all the croissants we ate*

1

I check my phone for the hundredth time in five minutes.

But given the fact that the plane is doing that terrifying circling thing right before landing and I'm no longer on the unreliable airline-provided internet, nothing has changed. There are no new messages or missed calls, only the repetitive warning from my music app that I'm on airplane mode.

I mentally will the plane back to the ground. As much as I enjoy being a backseat driver, something tells me the pilot won't hear me through the impenetrable door that separates first class from the cockpit.

Looking at the time moving slowly on the front of my phone makes me itchy, so I huff and drop it back on my lap. The stale, cold air makes this experience even more uncomfortable, but at least it's stopping my legs from sticking to the leather seat.

Why is it that delays only happen on the days I have somewhere to be?

I cross my arms and pin my hands down, forcing my

gaze on the squiggly lines of road and green tree tops on the ground that are finally getting bigger, indicating that we're close to landing. I was too antsy to appreciate the views until now, which is a sign of my own inner torment as well as my own privilege at spending way too much time in airplanes for the past decade.

When the plane finally touches down, I'm the first off.

I curse the Pittsburgh airport for the long walk and shuttle situation. Out of all the places I've been, I think this is the only airport with a random dinosaur statue in the middle of a row of escalators, and I do find it slightly endearing.

Once I'm through the point of no return, I dig my sunglasses and hat out of my purse. They're a flimsy shield that I pretend helps me blend into the background while knowing that a person wearing sunglasses inside likely does more harm than good.

Still, I'd rather not have my tired eyes photographed.

I collect my bag from the carousel and feel more in control of the clock, even though the state of traffic is completely out of my hands.

A man stands near the exit, holding a sign with "Olivia O" on it, and I roll my eyes.

Leave it to Adam, my manager, to publicly announce my arrival back into my home state. I should have come up with a better alias, something more vague, but I recognize that "Thirty-Year-Old Singer Who Is Dreading Her Return" would not have sufficed.

"Miss Olivia," he says with wide eyes and a smile.

I nod and shake his hand.

He insists on rolling my oversized checked bag for me,

2

and I let him. It's easier to keep my head down if I'm not trying to drag a heavy piece of luggage behind me. My gaze stays locked on the back of his shiny black shoes as he leads me through the small crowd of people toward the sleek black town car.

A few flashes go off before I close the door. The windows are tinted enough that I can see, thankfully, it's just a few middle-aged women who can barely work their smartphones and not professional paparazzi with high definition to pick apart my every flaw. I sigh in relief.

When I slink back into my seat, I notice one of those scented trees hanging off the rearview mirror that always gives me a headache, so I ask him if he minds if I roll down the window slightly. He doesn't, and thankfully, the rest of the forty-minute ride is quiet, aside from the low AM radio noise from the stereo.

I resume the terrible game of staring at my clock, but now that I have cell service again, I also get to mix in hate comments from my social media accounts and emails from people who all want something from me.

It helps distract me from the fact that the delay in take-off and landing made me late. Very late.

I like to be one of those people who shows up perpetually fifteen minutes early, even when you're supposed to show up "fashionably late" to something. But I'm here for Scott, who has never ever asked me for a favor, even after all he has done for me, and I'm frustratingly late.

In the nearly fifteen years that I've known him, Scott Davis's focus has been on making himself and everyone around him better. I didn't ask to be taken under his wing, even when he was my freshman year English teacher, but

3

he wedged his way into my life, and now I couldn't imagine being without him.

He's kind, funny, blunt as hell, and as selfless as I could have ever asked for in a mentor, so when he called me a few months ago and asked if I could introduce him at an event and maybe say a few nice things about him, I agreed before he even finished the question.

"Now wait just a minute," Scott chuckled, pushing back on my immediate response. "I haven't even told you anything about what you're agreeing to. Don't go all in on something before you know the details. How many times have I told you that?"

To be fair, he usually gives me that line in reference to business deals and big life decisions, but I guess it applies here, too.

Scott is one of the few people in my life who doesn't walk on eggshells in my presence. It's not just because of our relationship, though—he's never afraid to tell somebody how it is.

I smiled, even though he couldn't see it. "I'll save that energy for when I'm battling dealmakers and lawyers, Scott," I told him. "Not you."

He hummed into the phone. "But at Christmas, you mentioned some big fancy tour in June, and I just wanted to double-check that the dates don't clash."

"That *was* the plan," I admitted.

When I filled him in on the year's schedule at Christmas, it was assumed that I would be in the final stages of preparing for an album release, agonizing over every line and note. The label wanted me to run through the summer festival circuit, teasing new songs and testing out setlists before starting another official tour of my own in September.

I missed deadline after deadline, and the calls from my manager moved from polite nudges to frantic one-sided conversations. My schedule, and a large portion of Adam's, hinged on cranking out new music. The only problem was that I had no desire, passion, or inspiration for writing or creating anything.

My label used my lack of productivity against me, refusing to schedule more shows, the main and most lucrative way artists like me make money, until I sent them a round of demos.

I wasn't sabotaging myself on purpose or out of laziness, but regardless of many times I attempted to explain it to Adam, he wasn't buying it.

No matter how much I pushed myself to make something flow from my fingertips while sitting in the small studio in my condo, nothing good happened. Using brute force to spur art rarely works, so I tried meditating, solo dance parties and singalongs, writing whatever came into my mind, but it was still all crap.

It was almost as if my brain was blocked and my creativity was on strike, refusing to produce any longer until it was cared for, nurtured, and appreciated.

It was the driest of dry spells I've ever experienced in my life, and this one couldn't be solved with tequila and a one-night stand.

"But things have changed?" Scott clarified.

I sighed. "I don't have anything planned for June," I told him.

"Great!" he said, unable to hide his excitement.

I couldn't bear to disappoint him with the reason I had a rare scheduling gap.

"You know, this award is kind of like my version of the Grammys," he joked. "The Western Pennsylvania Teaching Society almost has the same notoriety as The Recording Academy, don't you think?"

"Definitely," I agreed.

My eyes flickered over to the gold-plated trophy, coated in a layer of dust, on my bookcase. Scott was one of the people I thanked in my acceptance speech when I picked up the Best New Artist award at age nineteen.

"So what kind of event is this?" I asked, turning the conversation back to him. "A big black-tie gala with passed appetizers and champagne?"

"If so, I'm not going," he said with a chuckle.

I doubted that a teaching society had money for either of those things, but I loved to tease Scott for this stance against formalwear. He was notoriously under-dressed for all things in life, claiming that life wasn't worth living unless he was comfortable, and for him, it almost always involved a threadbare shirt with a Pirates logo on it.

"I swear you're allergic to anything that's not cotton and denim…"

"You wouldn't be wrong," he admitted.

We talked for a little bit longer. He caught me up on the semester so far and his more ornery students, and I told him about my vocal exercises and a book I'd been reading when he called.

Before we jumped off so he could get prepared for his next class, he shared all the details he knew, with a promise to send anything else that came up so I could let the appropriate parties know.

I debated on whether I should even bother telling Adam the plan because it would open up *another* discussion of why I was tanking my career so spectacularly and not going on tour, but ultimately, I was glad I did.

One of his many assistants called me last week to let me know that they changed the plane for my flight and it adjusted their seating map; it was the reminder I needed to start packing.

Now, we're almost at the high school, and I take a minute to look over the speech I prepared. I scribbled it on a napkin between plane-sized glasses of wine. Even amid the worst writing slump of my life, I think it's an okay speech, or at least, worthy of how much Scott has meant to me over the years.

My school looks the same as the last time I had my eyes on it. The building itself is nondescript, a standard midwestern high school with two stories, dreary brown brick, and an oversized parking lot.

It's funny how after all this time I still remember where Maddy and I parked every single day of senior year, when the beat-up, second- or third-hand Camry was feeling cooperative enough for us to not have to take the bus.

Back then, I swore with my whole heart that I would never return.

I wanted nothing to do with this town and the people in it aside from Scott and Maddy, my childhood best friend— sometimes, my mom earned inclusion in that small group.

Aside from a few bouts of nostalgia here and there, I repressed as much of the first eighteen years of my life as I could. To say I don't have fond memories of Hill High School is the understatement of the decade.

I take a breath and will away the overwhelming sense of dread as we pull up to the front entrance.

"Do you mind taking my bags to my home address?" I ask the driver, fishing out a few twenties from my wallet.

He accepts the cash graciously, then confirms my address and punches it into his GPS.

"Miss Olivia," he says, catching me before I open the door.

I turn back to him and catch his sheepish expression.

"Do you mind taking a picture?"

"Of course not," I say, but I actually very much do mind.

The last thing I want to do is stop and take a photo when I'm all out of whack from traveling and running late. No, I take that back because the actual last thing I want is to be back in Hill.

Still, I lean forward to fit into the frame of his front-facing camera. The perception is all skewed from this angle, and I hope that this doesn't end up getting shared onto my timeline a few hundred times. If I'm lucky, he'll just show the picture to his wife or his niece or whoever in his family.

Most of the car services that Adam's company contracts with has a discretion clause and NDA, explicitly stating that no pictures, recordings, or details pertaining to passengers are permitted. I don't know if this guy is just ignoring it or if it doesn't exist.

I'm a little uncomfortable with the idea that I just sent a strange man with all of my personal belongings off to my house—where my mother is undoubtedly fuming that I missed dinner with her—but I have to trust that even if he's a rule-breaker, he's not some sort of super stalker.

I shake the thought off and redirect my focus back to putting one foot in front of the other before I open the door and dive right into the past.

When I step inside, everything is familiar enough to be surreal.

I force myself to blink to make sure that I'm seeing reality and not a memory or a nightmare. The walls are still the same off-white. The lights are too yellow. The trophy case is organized in the same haphazard chaos, but there are a number of additions.

It's a good sign that I haven't missed the ceremony entirely when I see a few people in the lobby. They were meandering about until I caught their attention, and they're all currently gawking at me and whispering to each other. I arrogantly think it's because of who I am but quickly realize it's because I'm wearing a ballcap and sunglasses inside, and they're all dressed up in cocktail attire.

I grab a program and dash into the bathroom to hide and freshen up. I step into the bathroom with faded blue tile, the ones I stared at a number of times during my four years of high school as I tried to force myself not to cry.

In some ways, I feel like the exact same person I was back then, even though I've toured the globe and had almost every success and failure imaginable happen to me.

I sigh at my reflection. I hoped for some time at home with a flat iron before coming here, but even though the air traffic gods were unkind to me today, it appears the vanity gods are still somewhat on my side.

I take a few minutes to smooth out the lines of my simple black dress and refresh my make-up. I'm a little underdressed compared to the others in the lobby, and I could wring Scott's neck for it. I didn't expect a gala, but I'm clearly not in cocktail attire—at the very least, I'm going to match his level of non-dressed-up.

It's not the best I have ever looked, but years of being on the road means that I don't show up as haggard as I did early in my career.

My stylist-for-hire would likely kill me for not wearing heels with this dress, but my beige pointed-toe loafers were what I slipped on hastily when I left my place in Los Angeles early this morning.

Pre-recorded peppy music comes over the loudspeaker, and I double-check the program, relieved that there is another award and a brief presentation before I need to be on stage for Scott. I give myself another few minutes to gather my courage, and even then, I don't have to full-out sprint around to the back door of the auditorium to get prepared.

I text Scott to let him know I'm here and hiding backstage.

My phone beeps, flashing a notice that my battery is below twenty percent. I despise that little red zone at the top right of my phone, and my irritation is heightened when I dig through my purse, coming up empty-handed. I stupidly stuffed my charger in my suitcase that, hopefully, is now at my house.

"Shit," I breathe out, elongating the word in a satisfactory way.

It's a small annoyance, all things considered in the

world, but it's just another thing piling onto this day. Being back in this building is enough of a mind-fuck that I would have loved something to help me get my bearings, even just a momentary distraction on social media to feel normal.

I step farther into the backstage area. I haven't set foot on this stage since the Christmas performance for Chorus during my sophomore year, and just like I did back then, I peek through the curtains.

The room is so packed that it's standing room only in the back.

Scott joked on the phone that this was a big deal, but I didn't take him seriously until now.

I'm flushed with pride over him and happy that he is finally being recognized. Scott is one of those teachers who is always at the top of students' favorite-of-all-time lists because he balances sternness and boundary pushing with entertainment and a general sense of coolness about him. Maybe it's his calm demeanor, or maybe I'm just biased.

Either way, I don't even want to try to add up the long hours of endless grammatical corrections and years of encouraging students to find their own voices—but I know Scott considers it time well spent.

I rub the edge of the worn, red velvet curtain in my fingertips as I scan the room for Scott. Luckily, he's in the first row, making it easy to pick him out.

Emotion swells in my chest as I see the content expression on his features. His hands lay folded neatly in his lap, emphasizing his general patience with the world around him, as he actively watches the presentation on stage.

I smile, but it fades when I see the empty seat beside him, likely saved for me.

He's one of those people who actually turns off their phones when asked to, so I doubt he received my text message; I hope he doesn't think I'm blowing him off.

"Um, excuse me?" The voice behind me belongs to a pimply teenager.

He holds a clipboard and shifts nervously until I release the curtain to meet his gaze. I see the recognition hit him, and he stands up exceptionally straight.

"Oh, damn," he says, ripping off his over-the-ear headset that probably weighs more than he does. "You're Olivia O."

"I am," I admit, clinging to a cool mask of politeness while he sputters, but I don't necessarily have the patience for him to get it together. "Do I need to get mic'd up?"

I glance around and answer my own question. The podium on the other side of the curtain has a microphone on it, and it's currently occupied by the man giving a presentation.

"How much longer until I'm up?" I ask, hoping he can actually be helpful.

"You've got about five minutes," another voice says from behind me.

I turn to see a teacher I recognize from my school days, but I can't remember her name. I never had her as a teacher, but I was pretty sure Maddy took a class with her. German, maybe. Or one of the sciences.

"Thank you," I say graciously. "Anything else I need to know?"

She shakes her head, but when she smiles, it takes over everything else. "Olivia Ott, it is so wonderful to see you back in the building."

I can't tell if she's just being polite or if she really means it. Is it so great for me to be back here? I'm sure they're getting some sort of publicity out of it, but I don't know how it impacts her directly.

"Or should I only call you Olivia O?" she adds quickly.

My smile stays put, but I cringe internally.

When I uploaded my first song to YouTube as a teenager, it was a cute moniker. My mom was super skeptical of the internet at the time, warning me against chatrooms and talking to strangers, and I knew she would feel better if I didn't put my last name on there, even if she never saw it.

Obviously, I was unaware of how that one song would turn into a country-wide phenomenon, and more than ten years later, I'd still be called it.

"Olivia is fine," I assure her.

She extends a hand, and I shake it quickly. When we break, she gestures for me to follow her, leading me behind the curtain to the other side of the stage.

The emcee clears his throat directly into the mic before he starts speaking. "The Western Pennsylvania Teaching Society is proud to welcome our next presenter to the stage. Although she needs no introduction in this town, I doubt I will get another chance to introduce a Grammy Award–winning artist, so I'm going to enjoy it."

The audience laughs.

I'm used to the attention by now, but I shift uncomfortably because I already know how the rest of this introduction is going to go, a rehashing of my career and tying it back to this crap town.

I roll my eyes. This night is about Scott, not me.

"While *Rolling Stone* has praised her 'soul-crushing lyrical originality,' I have it on good authority that she was actually failing freshman-level English until a man sitting in the front row intervened."

Again, the audience eats this up.

I stay completely still and don't react to his words, even though it's just the teacher and the teenager backstage with me who would witness any reaction.

"She has since gone on to become the youngest artist to hit more than one billion views on YouTube, among her many other accolades. Her first album, 'The Ever-Present Alabaster Moon,' was a multi-platinum critical success, and her first single, 'The Mourning After,' is still a radio hit to this day. All that said, we're lucky to have her here tonight. Please join me in welcoming Olivia O!"

2

The applause and cheers ramp up. I get a nod of encouragement from the teacher to make my way on stage, and I do.

The audience screams for me so loudly, it's almost as if I have won the award. I shake the hand of the emcee and step up to the podium, where Scott's award sits ready for me to hand off to him. It's a glass plaque in the shape of an apple with his name and other lines of text engraved on the base.

As my eyes adjust to the spotlight, I smudge a big thumbprint on the front of it. I drop my hands by my side and lean closer to the wood podium.

My eyes land on Scott, who is the reason I am here at this moment but here in the greater sense of the word.

The emcee's spiel did nothing for me, but I can tell from this distance that Scott's getting emotional about it. His heart is as big as it is soft—I'm pretty sure I've seen him cry more times than my own mother.

The roar dies at the same second I realize my notes are in a crumpled heap in my purse.

It was probably crap anyway, so I shake it off and feed off the energy of the room as best I can. Some things are better crafted in the moment, and this just might be one of them.

"Thank you all," I begin, encouraging the last few claps to fade out. "It is a tremendous honor to be here tonight as a guest of the prestigious Western Pennsylvania Teaching Society to honor Scott Davis."

My natural inclination is to speed through it, but I force myself to take a breath and slow down, wanting the words recognizing Scott to register with every single person in the audience.

"That story about me failing English during my freshman year, while somewhat embarrassing, is very true. I always struggled with reading and writing, but I was a, um, thrifty student, to put it delicately, who always managed to scrape by with a passing grade. Well, that worked for me until Scott Davis came along with his crusade of memorization and grammar tricks to help get me back on track. Without his diligence, I would probably still be taking that class and trying to pass it to this day," I joke, earning soft laughter from the audience. "Scott likes to refer to me as his most successful success story, and I can assure you that without him, there would be none of those accolades that were so kindly spoken about a moment ago."

I smile at the emcee and then take in the wave of cell phones pointed at me, recording this speech. It's a weirdly personal tribute to make a splash on the internet, but I don't think I can attend any public event or place without it ending up on YouTube.

Funny enough that the same platform that helped launch my career is now one I curse regularly.

"Scott saw a struggling student and jumped in to help during a time that his wife was battling cancer and gas prices were at an all-time high, but you wouldn't have known about his struggles just by talking to him. He's one of those people who sees the good in every situation and helps pull the best from you, whether you're a student, a friend, a colleague, or lucky enough to sit beside him during the hours-long wait at the DMV."

I'm overanalyzing every word I say, which is exactly what every PR person and speech coach I've worked with says not to do, but I can't help it.

When I'm performing a song, I dig deep and share a piece of my soul with the audience, drowning out all the nerves and chatter in my own mind, but speaking in front of crowds, trying to say things that will impress people and get my point across, makes my palms sweat.

I angle myself toward my former teacher and forever mentor, wanting to say the next lines directly to him, but I barely stifle a gasp when I lock eyes with the person sitting a row behind him.

Noah Washington.

Noah fucking Washington.

My instinct is to retreat back into my inner-teenager, to borrow those giant headphones from the kid backstage and escape into music, but I can't. There are about two thousand pairs of eyes on me, and for some reason, the only ones I can pick out belong to the man who made it his mission to make my life miserable in high school.

Fuck.

I force myself to swallow the panic and compose myself as best I can.

"I was a little lost when I was a teenager. I mean, at that age, who isn't filled to the brim with existential dread and hopeless despair as they deal with the social constructs created in an environment made up of raging hormones? Right?" I take a breath to slow the hell down. "But for me personally, Scott seeing something in me, my own suppressed imagination possibly, and helping me channel it into something productive...well, it changed everything for me."

I say these words directly to him, and it feels good to publicly recognize him in front of his peers and students.

"Without Scott, I don't know where I would be today, and that's the truth." My voice shakes with emotion. "There are so many amazing teachers here tonight, many of whom aren't aware of the influence they have on the lives of their students. I, for one, am proud to say that every single shred of praise or accomplishment I've had in my own life belongs to Scott as well, and I'm so damn proud of you, Scott."

I hold up the award and gesture to him. "I'm glad that somebody finally had the right idea to give you one of these. Come on up and accept this, Teacher of the Year."

He stands slowly and heads to the stage as the room breaks out into applause. I'm pulled into a big bear hug against his chest while he murmurs that he loves me, then

I make my way down the stairs to take the seat he saved for me.

I'm so caught up in the moment with Scott that I'm jarred once again when my eyes land on Noah fucking Washington, who grins at me.

I can't believe he has the audacity to *grin* at me.

All of the weepy emotion bubbling to the surface ceases to exist. My body, instead, floods with shaky rage and nerves. I have to remind myself that I am a successful person who got the hell out of this town and away from him. But looking at him makes me fall right back into old habits.

Somewhat ungracefully, I slump into the seat as a few people around me whisper hello and congratulations on such a powerful introduction. I smile and mouth my gratitude in return.

Noah is silent, but I can feel his presence behind me, which pisses me off even more.

I worked hard to purge the knowledge of his existence from my brain years ago, and now, he's all-encompassing. I wish he got fat or bald or grew some sort of deformity, but I begrudgingly accept he's an even better looking version of himself. Him and his stupid innocent *grin*.

"Thank you, Liv," Scott says into the microphone.

I will myself to ignore the memories of Noah's attitude and actions that flood my mind.

Scott is a little pale and shaky at the podium, and I chalk it up to nervousness. I assume being in a room with this many people is a different beast than standing in a classroom of thirty fourteen-year-olds talking about stanzas and independent clauses.

Writers never truly like being the center of attention. We're all introverts forced to become extroverts when our craft is recognized, which is what we need to survive but is kind of the exact opposite of what we actually want.

The truth is that despite Scott's best efforts, I'm not the best writer. I'm not the best singer either.

But somehow, people gloss over both of those facts because it's the combination that manages to gut people. At least, that's what I read in a magazine article once after my first album dropped.

I eventually learned the hard way to stop reading about myself, as tempting as it can be to do so.

My moderate talent aside, I have some clout, but I'm not super mainstream famous, like the type that sells out stadiums and has a picture on every magazine. I do have somewhat of a loyal following who likes the sound of my voice and the electronic music that I create to go along with it.

But part of my stardom, that I didn't want and didn't earn, was from my very publicized failed marriage to Jordan Gravers, who picked up the NBA Rookie of the Year Award the same year I earned my Grammy. I get recognized at least once with every outing regardless of which city I am in, but the attention increases when Jordan's in the news for something and the paps hound me, looking for a clip or quote of me reacting while I'm trying to buy a smoothie or doing some other banal task.

I exhale, and for the first time, I am very glad to be in a suburb north of Pittsburgh and away from the craziness of Los Angeles. I usually dread these trips. It's not because I don't want to see Scott or my mom, but the idea of being back here is so suffocating that I can't wait to be jetting off elsewhere.

The payments from an album release and summer tour would have been nice, but being here to bask in Scott's recognition is nearly priceless to me.

Scott finishes up his speech to a roar of applause, and I hug him again when he returns to our row.

"You're a rockstar," I tell him, which makes him grin from ear to ear.

I cling to his arm as the program continues with a guest speaker who rambles on about educational psychology for thirty minutes.

There's an audible sigh of relief when the emcee gets the mic back and encourages us all to stick around for drinks at the reception.

"Drinks?" I ask, raising an eyebrow.

"Drinks," Scott confirms with a nod.

We head back out to the lobby, which has been converted into a reception area. There are platters of cold cuts, fruit, and cheese, but as hungry as I am, the unrefrigerated spread doesn't look appetizing.

Scott and I are the first up to the bar, and we both order beers, something local and light.

"Cheers to you, Scott Davis, Teacher of the Year," I say after I drop a twenty in the tip jar.

We clink bottles.

I take a sip, appreciating the extra hoppy flavor. "I didn't know we were allowed to drink on school property."

He shrugs and fiddles with the label. "Must be because there's a *celebrity* in our midst."

"Where?" I demand and look over my shoulder, which makes him laugh.

More people file in, so instinctively, we both shuffle over to a corner away from the crowd.

Still, we spend the next hour getting cautiously or excitedly approached by people who ask me a barrage of questions. I try to steer the conversation back to Scott and his award. Most of the time, it doesn't work, but the beer on an empty stomach makes me a little warm and conversational.

I'm nearly finished with my third bottle as the man at the makeshift bar yells for last call. Scott and I both do a terrible job of not showing that we're relieved.

"I think this is my chance to sneak out, Liv," Scott whispers.

"What? No pictures or further public displays of your brilliance?" I tease.

"They did that all before," he admits, grimacing at the reminder. "It was…a long process. I'm glad you missed it."

He pulls me into a quick side hug, and I fall easily into it.

"You're sticking around for a few days, right?" Scott double-checks.

My appearances back here are usually spare and brief, but this time, I decided to stay longer. At the very least, it would be a good distraction from all the pressure and "encouragement" from my label about how badly I'm failing these days.

I nod. "A week."

"Come by for breakfast once you have some time with

your mom," he says, well aware of the delicate relationship with her I have to manage.

"Okay," I agree.

He breaks out into a full-on smile before we separate, him to the parking lot and me to the bathroom.

As I'm drying my hands, I dig for my keys in my purse, only to remember that I'm not in Los Angeles and I do not have my car here with me. I forgot to ask the driver to come back and pick me up after he dropped my stuff off at the house.

I groan, and the volume of it increases when I pull out my phone, which is now completely dead. I try to turn it on again just for the hell of it, but it doesn't come back to life. All I can see is my unhappy face staring back at me, reflecting off the blank screen.

As I'm about to go around and beg someone with a charger, I hear the voice of a very enthusiastic stage mom who talked my ear off for twenty minutes about how fabulous her daughter is and would I please, please, please share her music with some executives?

I didn't have the heart to tell her that my current music executives don't give a shit about my opinion on anything unless it's my next record, so I just deflected and managed to escape the conversation.

Before she enters the bathroom, I rush into one of the stalls and hide. She tells another woman all about the conversation with me and won't shut up about how I'm going to probably do a duet with her daughter at a Super Bowl someday.

I wait a full ten minutes after they're gone just to make

sure I don't have a chance of getting trapped in conversation again.

The parking lot is nearly empty when I finally step outside the building. It's a cool, beautiful June night, and I'm encouraged by the beers I downed that walking home is a great idea. It's not like I have any other options at this point.

I know the route well. Maddy and I drove on it every day for years, and if I remember correctly, I think it's about a twenty-minute drive to my house. I try to do the math in my head to figure out how long it would take me to walk compared to driving, and I give up.

It will be great exercise, I tell myself, and it's so nice to be out on my own and appreciate the stars without the light pollution from the crowded city. The air is so clean, maybe I'll try to catch some lightning bugs in my hands on the way home.

Yes, this is a great idea. I stretch my arms upward and try to walk in a straight line. Was it three or four beers I had, now that I think about it?

I shake it off. I don't care because I'm living in the present and letting go of all the stresses from the west coast. I'm just a woman on a long walk, just like any other woman who goes for a walk. I start laughing and continue moving my feet forward.

I'm so deep in my own head that I don't even hear the rumble of a car pull up to the sidewalk.

My bubble bursts as a gravelly voice asks, "Need a ride?"

I nearly jump out of my own skin at the sound, and when I glance down at who wants to save me from miles of nothing but road and my own thoughts, all of the air whooshes out of my lungs.

It's Noah.

Noah Washington.

Noah fucking Washington.

3

I can't pinpoint the exact day the torment started, but I remember the first time I felt completely defenseless.

Our freshman year.

Football season.

Maddy wants to go to a game, even though I can barely keep up with the rules of the sport, because she says it's one of those high school rites of passage we should experience.

She and I squeeze into the bleachers in the student section, among the hundreds of red and gold painted faces. We scream for three full quarters even though we couldn't care less about the outcome of the game. We just want to have fun, to feel included, and it's working.

With ten minutes left of the game, I venture down the bleachers and toward the snack bar. I have enough change in my pocket to get one can of pop. These days, Dr Pepper feels like an indulgence. My mom and I, being on a tight grocery budget, strictly drink tap water and milk.

I stand in the underbelly of the bleachers, not caring that the stomping of feet on the metal ricochets into my ear drums, and pop open the can. I smile as I take that first sip, letting the spicy cherry and vanilla flavors wash all over my tongue.

Suddenly, I'm off balance.

Someone's hands are on my waist, pushing me backward until my back slams against one of the poles.

I know who it is without even looking up.

"What are you doing, Noah?" I ask.

I stopped growing two years ago, but Noah's shooting up every time I look at him, which is more often than I like. He towers above me by at least six inches. His stature alone is intimidating enough, but the anger rolling off him in waves only contributes to my panic and discomfort.

Our position shields us from the people milling around, socializing instead of watching the game.

He's close to me, as close as someone could be without actually touching another human being, and I can see the pure venom in his eyes.

I need to be more alert, I realize, because it appeared that he's only getting started with whatever game he is playing, and I don't know the rules.

What did he want from me?

Why was he so angry?

What was happening?

I have so many questions, and I have already cried so many tears over this situation. I don't want to shed any others in his presence, so I fake it.

I pretend to not be terrified when he rips the can from my hand and throws it behind him with no regard for repercussions. I pretend that everything is going to be fine and this would be over soon, and I *would never think about him again. I will away the rest of my time in high school because of him.*

"What are you doing, Noah?" I ask again, but this time, instead of fear, I try to make my voice sound as bored as I can, as if his challenging me didn't bother me at all.

He leans even closer to me.

If I tilted up my head, our lips would meet, but I don't dare do that. I grind my teeth and lock his eyes, waiting to see what his next move will be.

"Whatever the hell I want," he says, and I swear that the hot breath of his words and the ghost of his lips touched mine when he said it.

Just as quickly as he appeared, he's gone.

I stay rooted in place until the scoreboard counts down the final seconds of the game.

From my vantage point, I see that same stadium in the distance. The lights project into the sky even though it's ten o'clock in June and there are no gym classes or sporting events happening on the field.

The question he asked goes unanswered because the audacity of him to pull up beside me and ask it with such innocence is nearly beyond comprehension.

I'm almost stunned at having a reaction for this situation, so I do the most pathetic thing my buzzed mind can come up with at the moment—turn away and not even acknowledge his existence.

It's petty, and it's a defensive move, but it works until the beige pointed-toe loafers that I silently praised earlier betray me.

The hard leather rubs against the backs of my heels in a repeated torture that is definitely blistering further with each step I take. I try to pull the socks up mid-stride, but they're the no-show kind, and they're not budging. Damn useless pieces of fabric.

"To hell with it," I mumble, wrenching off one shoe at a time and shoving them roughly into my purse.

The backs of my heels thank me by not bleeding all over the sidewalk.

"Hey, did you hear me?" Noah calls.

I hate how deep his voice is.

It's too alluring, and if it didn't belong to someone who I hated so wholly, I would want to listen to it, have conversations with it, hear it laugh and...oh shit, he's following me.

The car moves at a ridiculously slow pace. I thought my power walk was fast, but I bet he's not even pushing on the gas.

Why didn't I take up marathon running instead of singing and songwriting?

"You probably don't remember me, but I'm—"

"I remember," I practically spit at him.

The anger is so visceral, I couldn't stop myself if I tried.

Did he think I could easily forget all the shit he and his friends put me through for four goddamn years of my life? The jokes, pranks, and humiliation? My plan to not pay any attention to him is a total failure, and I'm angry at myself and him for having to endure this.

"Right."

I imagine he is thinking about all the same stuff I am, but from his own perspective.

The upper hand is a glorious thing to have, I guess. I wouldn't know.

I resume walking with a renewed sense of purpose. Getting away from Noah and into more alcohol or my bed is what I put at the forefront of my mind.

"So you're really going to walk all the way home?" Noah asks.

From my peripherals, I can see how relaxed he is. Seat reclined, one arm on the steering wheel, the other halfway out the window, catching the summer air in his fingertips.

His relaxed stature annoys me just as much as his grin did earlier.

For the next ten minutes, he continues that slow pace in his car, while I'm walking as fast as I can to get away from him. The longer this continues, the more I sweat and breathe heavily.

I try to hide it, just like I always do when I'm exercising and the most out of shape in the class, but it's really difficult, and I'm thirsty as hell.

Noah, apparently sick of the silent treatment, turns up the volume on the radio.

I don't hate it, honestly. Very rarely am I in complete silence, and it's kind of nice that the radio station still has the same DJs after all these years. Their voices and nicknames are familiar to me.

Maddy and I used to sneak into the bathroom during school hours to call in and try to win tickets to concerts on our prepaid phones, but we were never successful.

I am maybe into my second mile when I hear my own voice on the radio.

Without a word, Noah cranks the dial.

It's one of my newer songs, "Frustrating to the Point of Unenjoyment," and the irony is not lost on me.

It's one of the most personal I've ever written, pulling words and notes from conversations with Jordan in some of our—thankfully very few—rough days. I once loved how fierce this song made me feel when I sang it with my eyes closed in a recording studio.

My inner thoughts, making up the first verse, taunt me.

> *It's a state of confusion, endlessly unsettling*
> *Talking in circles while the sun burns*
> *You face the clouds and ask why, how*
> *The sky doesn't answer but I think*
> *The pit in my stomach does now*
> *Because we're thriving off the past*
> *That fell through my grasp*
> *While we slipped our own minds*

I stop walking, putting my hands on my hips to drive my point home and catch my breath. "Turn it off," I demand.

He doesn't break eye contact as his pointer finger taps the touch screen, making it louder as the chorus picks up.

> *If I were more gentle*
> *But less fragile*
> *If I remained quiet*
> *While screaming*
> *If I became beautiful*
> *But kept the flaws*
> *You'd be happy*
> *And I'd be someone else*

It's baffling to me that after all this time, I'm just a game to Noah. This one little power move, among many, confirms it. As teenagers, I was the result of boredom or some weird internal power struggle he needed to prove to himself, but now, I don't understand his motive.

Does he want to pick right back up where things left off in high school? Him the bully and me powerless to stop it? It's been ten years for fuck's sake.

I'm no longer some meek teenage trailer park girl who cries herself to sleep because of his torture.

"Turn it the fuck off, Noah," I scream over and over again.

I completely lose my shit, banging my hands on the roof of his car. It's venomous or crazy enough that he jumps and actually complies.

I bite back this feeling of satisfaction as I walk again, and just when I think I've finally got him to leave me alone, his tires screech and he's once again on the road beside me.

"There's construction up ahead," Noah says lifelessly. "I had to take a detour earlier because of all the broken glass."

I stop and stare at my feet, wanting to weep at the idea of putting my shoes back on. I press my finger against the back of my heel and wince. I've arrived in Blister Town already.

There are not enough swear words in the universe right now to exemplify my feelings at this exact moment, so I put my dignity aside. Without looking at Noah, I sulk over to his passenger side and let myself in.

I buckle my seatbelt and try not to marvel at how normal his car is.

The Washingtons made a lot of money from illegitimate

sources under the guise of owning convenience stores and food manufacturing companies around the city.

Growing up, Noah didn't hesitate to flaunt his wealth, but for some reason, the car he drove now had to be about thirty thousand dollars cheaper than the one he and his friends used to do donuts in the parking lot with.

His eyes bore into my side profile, and I refuse to succumb to the urge to turn. The thought of looking at him and acknowledging his persistence and victory makes me want to get out and walk barefoot on the glass.

My posture stays rigid until he presses on the gas, expertly riding the curves of the Western Pennsylvania hills that I sometimes dream about at night.

Without asking permission, I crack the window, inhaling the summer air and ignoring the fact that I am a foot away from a boy who once encouraged the entire wrestling team to call me "Horse Face." I hadn't grown into my front teeth or figured out what haircut flattered my face shape yet. They filled my locker with sugar cubes and clomped down the hall after me between classes during the spring semester of my sophomore year.

Even now with whatever meager success I have to my thirty-year-old name, I still run my tongue over my front teeth self-consciously from time to time.

I catch my reflection in the side view mirror as we hit an intersection. It's hard to see at this time of night, but I tug at my hair, a blunt cut with ends that dip just below my shoulders.

Over Christmas, I dyed my mousy brown hair a silvery gray, hoping that a change in appearance would spur a change in myself. It didn't work, but I liked the color enough to keep it.

The humming sound of the engine cuts, and I blink and snap my gaze toward Noah.

"What's this?" I ask.

"My house," Noah answers indifferently, reaching for a shopping bag in the back seat.

We're in front of a neat row of townhouses. They're simple, brick-front and two stories, and I once again am surprised by this modesty.

Noah's family owns a huge property in the neighborhood at the edge of the school zone. I imagined it to be a haunted, horrible castle, but in reality, a lot of people got drunk and at least one girl got pregnant in high school at one of his infamous parties.

"I need to stop in really quick," he explains, as if that will subdue me.

"You couldn't do it after you dropped me off?" I'm being really ungrateful, but it's him, so I don't care.

He has the audacity to laugh, and of course, it's not kind. "I'll be in and out." His voice is lifeless. "Three minutes max."

I glance back at the property in front of me, and I hate that I'm interested enough to want to see inside. I'm hopeful that his life turned out horribly.

I need to see it for myself, so I take a page from his playbook and follow him without permission.

4

Noah's eyebrows raise, but he says nothing, simply twirling the bag in one hand as he unlocks the door with the other.

A bright, female voice calls for him.

Great.

Noah found someone who loves him and he can come home to every night. Someone who looked past all of his darkness and cruelty enough to be with him.

Then again, his cruelty was usually only directed toward me—from what I recall, he had no shortage of women asking him to the Sadie Hawkins dance every year.

I'm trying to decide if I want to see this woman for myself or go hide in the car, but my curiosity prevails. I follow him up the stairs and down the hallway, sneaking a peek at the kitchen, which is clean for the most part. There are just a few dishes and baby bottles precariously stacked on top of each other in the sink.

Bottles? I balk. Does he—is he a father?

The blood pounds in my ears.

Noah Washington…married with at least one child. My mind pictures Noah dating, falling in love, at the altar, on a honeymoon, in the delivery room, all the way up until this moment.

It's a fast montage, and it doesn't fit with everything I remember about him.

The flood of text messages is enough to make me regret even wanting a cell phone in the first place.

"U r ugly"

"Horse face"

"Why do you even exist"

"You are a waste of air"

I glance across the cafeteria to see Noah and his friends huddled together in laughter as they continue sending text messages about how stupid, ugly, and unaccomplished I am.

I'm going to have to get a ride to the store after school so I can see if the provider can block numbers…or I'll just have to change mine. I don't know how they got this number in the first place or how they are so fast at texting on the little keys.

I close my eyes and can't wait for lunch to be over.

How can someone like him possibly be responsible for a small human being?

Noah knocks on the door to the bedroom next to the kitchen. It's a weird gesture, considering this is his own house, and I can't speculate fast enough what the reason for this behavior is.

I stand as confidently as I can. On the inside, I'm a nervous wreck in anticipation of meeting Mrs. Noah Washington.

I'm still a little buzzed, but I definitely want his wife to be hideous or mean or maybe beautiful because he found a way to redeem himself. I hate him so much that it's all that consumes me in that moment until familiar black hair and green eyes overtake my vision.

"Liv?" Maddy wants to shriek, but she's holding a sleeping baby in her arms, so it's a forceful whisper. "Oh my gosh! What are you doing here?"

I blink a few times, trying to clear my vision, but the view stays the same.

My high school best friend married my high school bully, and they fucking *procreated*.

I'm speechless.

"Olivia needed a ride home," Noah says in a quiet clipped tone.

He gently takes the sleeping baby from her arms, and it's not an awkward motion. It's far from it, actually, like he has done it thousands of times, confirming my suspicion.

I now notice that diapers and formula are in the bag, and I feel like a total asshole for snapping at him about stopping here and bringing the bag in.

Maddy surprises me by throwing her arms around me and pulling me close. She's hugging me like things haven't changed at all since I last saw her.

I try to return it as best I can, but I'm still wrapping my head around the fact that she has shacked up with Satan incarnate.

She's looking at me expectantly, like I should say something, but I don't know what to say to her. I don't know who this person is standing in front of me, or who the man is whispering to a sweet sleeping child as he returns to the bedroom Maddy just exited.

"You had a baby." I state the obvious because it seems

like it's a safe thing to do even though I want to ask so many questions about what the hell led to all of these decisions.

She laughs, and it's as adorably obnoxious as I remember. There's a defined note of exhaustion to it, though, and I feel for her.

It's the understatement of the century that being a new mother is challenging, but at the very least, it seems like Noah is an active participant in co-parenting, which is more than Maddy and I can say for our own sets of parents.

Still, I can't believe she had these gigantic life events, and I lived my life in my own bubble, completely unaware of everything happening to her.

"Why didn't you call me?" I ask as Maddy takes me back to the kitchen.

"I didn't have your number anymore," Maddy answers. She's not angry or sad, just telling it like it is.

"Sorry about that," I wince. "I have to change it like every six months because my numbers always get posted on Reddit and then I get a bunch of prank calls, and it's a mess."

"Sounds like it." She tugs her hair into a pile on the top of her head and secures it with an elastic. "Can I offer you a drink?"

I'm dehydrated as hell from all the drinking and walking, and I gratefully accept a glass of water, downing half of it in one gulp.

Maddy grabs a can of pop for herself from the fridge, and I'm glad it's not Dr Pepper or I would probably lose my shit for the full circle feeling of it all.

I have more time to process the little details around me.

In our tiny trailer growing up, we taped to-go menus to the fridge. My mom let Maddy and me color on the front of the cabinets with markers just so she could have some peace on a Saturday afternoon, and we practically drowned in stuff that we inherited from other people moving out.

This house is clean, but it looks like the furniture came with the place. I don't see a hint of personality or charm, which goes against everything I know about Maddy's style. She's bright and bubbly and could spend hours in the sale section at a home goods store, sniffing candles and brainstorming on how to redecorate a bathroom with a beach theme.

She sits down on a barstool, and I join her.

With her hair out of the way, I can see the dark circles under her eyes. She's always been thin, but now she looks frail.

"How old is...your baby?" I fumble with the words because I just want her to explain everything about her life and this new human she created.

"Liam is four months old." Her entire face lights up when she says this. "He figured out how to roll from his stomach to his back last weekend, and I cried."

I smile. "Sounds like he picked up some DNA from those gymnastics classes you dragged me to at the YMCA."

"Oh my gosh, I still have nightmares about those instructors." She laughs again. "Miss Peggy, right? She was vicious."

It's true, and it's one of the few good memories that has caught my attention in the past few hours. Maddy and I always managed to have fun together. No matter how awful school was for me or home life was for her, we had each other.

When my life blew up—in a good way, not a bad one— the summer after we graduated from high school, the label flew my mom and me out to Los Angeles. I signed a ton of papers, found a tiny room in a shared house, and by September, she left and I stayed.

Maddy and I kept in touch on social media and with the occasional phone call. I made it a point to see her whenever I returned. I offered to fly her out to see me a number of times, but she always had work or something else that prevented her from coming out.

For the last few years, my visits back were so brief that I essentially came back from the airport, stayed the night to visit my mom and Scott, and then I was out again. Over time, we lost touch.

"So you got married?" Maddy asks. "And then divorced."

She grimaces. It's not lost on me that she might be just as curious about me as I am about her.

I smile and take another sip of water before answering. "I did. Both of those things."

This is the exact point in the conversation that Noah comes back to hang in the doorframe. Not contributing to anything, just watching the two of us.

"It must be tough living a life where everyone picks you apart," Maddy says.

I shrug and look pointedly at Noah. "My high school bullies prepared me for that aspect."

His eyes darken. "Well, surely shacking up with an NBA

player was a good trade-off," he deflects, jabbing right back at me.

I almost laugh. New house, new car, new baby, but the same Noah is buried inside his rigid exterior.

"I can't believe you were married to Jordan Gravers," Maddy says with a smile, ignoring the glares and tension between Noah and me. "You, of all people, being with a professional athlete."

"Sometimes I can't either," I admit.

We were an unlikely pair and complete opposites in some ways, but I think he found my disinterest in his growing celebrity appealing. Adam, my manager, was actually the one who introduced us—they went to college together.

Jordan and I rushed to get married. At the time, it was all fun and new, but we were naive to all the challenges we had ahead of us.

We were both grateful that we had a relatively drama-free marriage and divorce, but with my touring and recording schedule and his team schedule, it felt like we were friends who occasionally hooked up rather than husband and wife.

His publicist told the media our split was amicable, and it was for the most part, a few fights here and there before we decided to go our separate ways. We even still text each other on Christmas and call each other to catch up every few months. Overall, we could have both done a lot worse and recognize it.

In the press, even to this day, we maintain a good rapport, only speaking the praises of each other—no matter how badly he loses a game or the critics slam my albums.

I try to figure out how to break the ice and ask about Maddy and Noah, but the baby begins what I assume is a full-body wail. "I need to get him down for the night," she says apologetically. "Will you come back tomorrow? Or can we meet somewhere?"

"Sure," I say, picking up a pen from the table to write my phone number down on a piece of junk mail.

It will give me time to clear the alcohol from my system and figure out how the hell to ask the questions I want answers to.

She gives me another hug before rushing back to the other room.

I chug the rest of my water and stand up, trying to keep my eyes on everything but Noah, but Noah only looks at me.

"Shall we?" he asks, watching me drop the cup in the sink.

I retreat to the car, and the entire time, his gaze stays on me.

Even with the windows open, I'm suffocated by his presence. It's too big, with too much history between us, to fit in this four-door sedan.

The ride is silent. Noah doesn't touch the radio, likely not wanting to risk hearing my voice or my anger again, and I realize too late that he's driving back to the trailer park where I grew up instead of the house I own now.

"Oh, actually, my mom doesn't live here anymore," I say, breaking the quiet.

I hate that I'm in this weird debt situation and that Noah is doing something nice for me. Well, it's surface-level nice because I haven't figured out the motive behind this, and while we're not clawing each other's eyes out, it's not exactly a comfortable feeling between us.

"Look, you don't have to keep up this charade any longer, Noah."

He side-eyes me. "Charade?"

I refuse to look at him because when I do, I'll lose my resolve to get out of this or completely lose my shit. I don't think either would be good for my friendship with Maddy.

I rub my temples with my fingertips, feeling the early onset of a hangover headache. I can't control that, but I can get myself out of this situation before it gets any worse.

"My phone is dead, so if you just let me borrow your charger or lend me your phone, I'll wait here for a cab to come."

I force myself to keep my gaze fixed on the road, so I don't see whatever emotion rolls over his face, but I do hear the very clear annoyance in his tone.

"You're in Hill, not LA," he reminds me. "It'll take forty-five minutes for the cab to get here. Just tell me where you need to go, and I'll take you."

I know he's right, but I still sigh when I resign to just try and get this over with. "Valencia Woods," I say quietly.

Noah nods and makes a U-turn, and once again, we zoom along in complete silence.

I want to regret accepting this stupid ride, but to erase Noah from the evening would mean I lose my unexpected reunion with Maddy. I didn't realize how much I needed a real friend until she pulled me into her arms.

Eventually, I'll need to move past the weird circum-stances because as much as I want to stab Noah in the eyeballs with a fork, I can't bear knowing Maddy is unhappy.

If she sees something in him, maybe I can, too.

My eyes move over to Noah's hands on the steering wheel, the only thing I permit myself to look at. He catches me shifting closer to him, and I jerk back against the seat.

"So what were you doing at the event tonight?" I blurt out, trying to sound casual.

For a second, it doesn't seem he's going to answer me, my first real attempt at a conversation between us now, maybe ever.

"My colleague gave the presentation after the awards." That one line is all I'm getting, I guess.

"You're a shrink, too?" I ask because now I'm fishing for information about his life and Maddy's.

"No," he says evenly. "We work in the same hospital."

I don't know why I'm forcing this conversation. It's a stupid idea, and his sharp tone seems to agree. He doesn't clarify beyond that, so I cross my arms and decide to keep my mouth shut, only speaking to give him directions.

I start to nod off but force myself awake by digging my nails into my scalp. I'm reinvigorated when he turns onto my street, and when we pull up to the house, I can't help but allow the happiness to bubble up inside me.

Maddy and I used to drive by this house and stare at it in awe, wondering if it was a mirage or if a house this sleek and beautiful could exist.

Its white stone exterior, gigantic windows, and painstakingly decorated interior were not things the previous owners parted with easily, but the house and my condo in Los Angeles are the only two big splurges I've bought with the money I'd made in my career so far.

When some people win the lottery, they blow it and end up poorer than they were before, but I've locked away my money in long-term savings accounts and modest investment accounts recommended by my financial adviser.

Noah clears his throat, and I snap out of my trance-like state. I've just been sitting here, staring at my own property. It's odd behavior, considering that all I want to do is get away from him. I would apologize, but I don't have it in me.

When I reach for the door handle, Noah's hand shoots to my wrist, pulling me back toward him. I'm stunned by how my body jolts, not by the surprise of the move but the heat in his gaze.

"What the fuck, Noah?" I sputter.

His grip is stronger than it used to be, but I manage to tear myself out of his grasp.

He puts his hands up in a defenseless motion, showing that he, at this moment, has no ill intentions. I don't believe him.

"It's been more than a decade, Noah," I say. "Ten fucking years, but you're still doing this to me."

Something flickers in his eyes, and I have to stop myself from reading into whatever it revealed about him. "Doing this to you?"

I pull at the ends of my hair. "Torturing me."

It's an honest admission, but it's a truth lodged so deep within me that I can't tell if I want to sob or puke when I let it go.

Noah sighs loudly. "I know you hate me, Olivia."

More like despise, but okay, I'm not going to argue semantics at this point.

"And you have every right to," he admits.

I can't tell if I'm more stunned by the fact that we are having this conversation or that the actual words came from his mouth, but he doesn't pause long enough for me to figure it out.

"But we're not teenagers anymore. When I look back on what I said, how I treated you, I can't believe I was capable of those things. I'm so sorry for everything I put you through. I wish I had a justification or a good reason for it other than my own shortcomings, but I guess I just want you to know I'm sorry. I know it doesn't take any of it back, but you deserve an apology."

I sit speechless.

I can tell by the despair that takes over his face and the way he rakes his fingers across the top of his skull, ruining his perfectly styled hair, that he is genuine. Or a really fucking good actor.

I try to hold onto the hate, to the years of torment that still feel very real, but I can't bring myself to resurface the anger. I'm exhausted by it.

I unbuckle my seatbelt and slink out of the car.

"Thanks for the ride," I choke out and slam the door.

5

After a restless night's sleep and big breakfast with my mother, I drive back over to Noah's townhouse. I'm a little jittery after three cups of coffee, but I'm also antsy to talk to Maddy.

The last eighteen hours have transported me to the past. As if my tossing, turning, and near-constant thinking of Noah wasn't enough of a reminder, sliding into the same beat-up Camry I drove in high school sure does it.

My hair is a little damp at the ends. I'm always too warm and impatient after my shower to fully dry it, so I roll down the windows to expedite the process. The warm early summer air whooshes through the car, and I want it to carry out all the negativity with it.

I regret letting the drama and heartache weigh down so heavily on me when I was younger, but now, as a fully formed adult, I still don't think I've moved past it.

Too much time has been spent caring about other people's opinions, and I need to reprioritize.

Instead of focusing on what I need to do and how to become the person I want to be, I get caught up in the minutiae of my feelings, and it's debilitating. I think it makes me a better writer but a less productive human.

Scott definitely told me a version of that while I was a teenager, but the words didn't hit until now.

Adam calls me and interrupts my brooding.

My gut reaction is to ignore the call like I normally would, but self-realization, aiming for maturity, and personal growth is a bitch.

"Double O," he says when I answer.

I hate that nickname, but he's the only person I let it slide with. I have to hold my phone up with one hand and drive with the other because I'm an idiot who never upgraded her car to something built in this decade with hands-free calling and a touch screen.

"Hey, Adam," I say. I try to sound cheerful, but it falls flat.

"Oh, wow, life's that good in Hell, Pennsylvania?"

He knows it's called Hill, but he insists on giving everyone and everything a nickname. My town earned that one after I broke down crying at an album release party and told him all about my tortured teenage years.

It stuck, and I haven't had vodka since.

"It's…"

"Hell?" Adam finishes.

I laugh, rolling up the windows so I can hear him more clearly.

"It kind of is, but it kind of isn't," I admit. "Just a lot of…stuff in the past getting dug back up."

"That sucks," he says.

"Yeah."

He clears his throat and pauses long enough for me to know whatever he's about to say is not going to be reassuring. The pleasantries portion of the conversation is over before it ever really got started.

"Look, O, I'm going to cut right to it," Adam says. "I know you wanted to stay for the week, but the label is demanding that you return A-S-A-P."

It's funny how powerful people like to "demand" things.

I'm not their puppet; I'm a person, and I think sometimes they forget that when looking at sales numbers and calendars.

"I don't have anything for them, and you know it," I say sadly.

He sighs. "I know, but I can't keep delaying this for you."

"Well, if they're that pissed, another few days won't hurt anything. I never come back here, and I think Scott is looking forward to spending a little more time with me."

Adam is silent, which means he's counting down from ten and trying not to strangle me through the phone. He has been with me since the beginning when I was sleeping in a van between gigs, and he has benefited greatly from my success.

"It's already been a few months," I continue. "Me coming there isn't going to change the truth—"

"They're talking about dropping you, O," Adam cuts in.

The blow is so devastating that I am glad I'm idling in the street outside Noah's place. I certainly would have veered off the road and crashed due to the shock.

"Fuck" is all I can say, and I do, elongating the word into a ten-second exhale.

"I'll move your flight up." That's all Adam can do for me at this moment.

"Okay," I mutter.

"Wish it didn't have to be like this, O, but you're going to have to come face the music yourself."

I hate that cliché. "Thanks, Adam."

"Talk to you later," he says before disconnecting the call.

I swallow and grip the steering wheel, digging my fingernails into the hard plastic material.

It's not like Adam hadn't warned me that this could happen; I just didn't want to hear it.

Being dropped from a label can be a career-ender, spurring all sorts of rumors that make artists untouchable. I unleash an inspired slew of curse words, letting the weight of it all out until I'm out of breath.

I fall forward, pressing my forehead down into my palms.

It's not that I wasn't trying to write. In fact, it was the exact opposite. I've tried to force it without success. I'm all done up inside after ten years of push, push, push from the label, my manager, the fans even. I'm proud of what I've accomplished, the art I've put into the world.

I just need a break, not a death sentence.

Tapping on the window scares the shit out of me, and I jump, nailing my elbow against the center console in the process. I'm one of those people who has mysterious bruises that show up at regular intervals without explanation, so I'm sure this one is going to be a dark purple by dinnertime.

I glance up at Noah.

His dark gaze is just confused enough to clue me into the fact that he just witnessed me yelling a string of profanity at my steering wheel.

The only thing that takes my attention away from the clusterfuck of my career is how form-fitting Noah's dark blue scrubs are. I don't remember any hospital staff filling out their v-neck shirt that way when I had my appendix removed a few years ago.

He steps back so I can snap out of it and let myself out of the car.

I smooth my still-wet hair back off my face. I'm wearing a wrinkled, oversized shirt dress and a pair of my mom's sandals. The only Band-Aids we had in the house were bright pink, a color I would never wear normally but my mother loves, and there are five on each foot covering all the blisters.

Feeling disheveled is off-putting enough as it is, but in the presence of Noah, it's unbearable.

"Everything okay?" he asks.

If I open my mouth, everything's going to spill out. He is the last person on earth I want to talk to right now, so I grit my teeth.

Maddy, my raven-haired savior, opens the front door and calls for me. "Livvy, come on in."

I swear the ghost of a smile crosses his face, finding satisfaction in my being upset, but it doesn't match up with the Noah I left the night before.

I can only assume that Maddy's happiness is the reason

he apologized, but it feels like a betrayal to her for me to acknowledge the pull I feel toward him.

I turn my back, tearing my eyes away from him. Maddy ushers me inside, and I proceed to spill my guts to her.

Over the years, I've gone through cycles of friends in LA —fellow new artists, basketball wives, producers—but I've never had the "all love and no judgment" feeling like I do with Maddy.

Even though we've been distant for a few years, she readily steps into the role of supporter and active listener.

Little Liam sits in a booster seat contraption attached to the counter, and he drools while he watches me with wide eyes. I'm sure even he can sense what a failure I am.

As I'm ranting at full speed, Maddy slides a box of tissues my way. I begin to calm down, and she feeds me snacks from the cupboard and a big glass of ice water. Maddy leans on her elbows, needing a minute to digest the half hour of near-constant venting.

She fluffs her bangs as she mulls over how to say the next sentence. "Would it really be the worst thing to happen?"

"Which part?" I ask.

Maddy bites back a smile. "Getting dropped from your label. And before you interrupt me, I know you keep throwing out words like 'career-ender' and 'never going to write again,' but do you really want to work for a company that is forcing you to do something you don't want to or can't do right now? You're a person, Liv, not a machine."

I take a big sip of water.

This is the Maddy I've known and loved throughout my life. Compassionate to a fault, but sharp and solution-oriented. I appreciate it, but I'm not sure if she understands the complications of being an unsigned artist again.

Record labels have big budgets for promotions, branding, marketing, distribution, legal work, and probably fifty thousand other things I'm not aware of. It's a daunting task to take on alone. The label has been with me since I went viral on YouTube as a teenager, and they put me on a continued trajectory upward.

"Just take some time to think about it," she adds gently. "Yes, you'd lose a lot, but think of all you could gain. Complete control of your own time, with no one breathing down your neck to produce. Besides, aren't there a good number of artists who have their own labels now? Or just publish independently? I'm not the most up to date with this kind of stuff."

She glances at Liam, who sucks on one of his fingers.

If I had a little Liam, I sure as shit wouldn't care about what's happening in the music industry, but here she is, full of empathy for me.

I swallow. "I'm so sorry, Maddy. I feel like I just came into your life like an emotional tornado and destroyed everything in my path."

Liam starts to coo. Maddy picks him up, jutting out the side of her hip to hold him against it.

"Oh stop it. Liam and I both love the company. Sometimes we get lonely during the day, don't we?"

The smile on my face is unexpected, given all the other emotions pouring out of me, but it's very welcome.

"It's nice to feel needed sometimes," she admits.

I can understand that, I suppose, with Noah doing whatever he does at the hospital. Liam is still very attached to her, but getting adult time is probably a good thing. Maddy and I were both never really big social creatures other than with each other or when forced to be in school.

It's time to shift the focus over to her, and I'm going to start with the biggest bomb of them all. "So when did you and Noah get together?"

I drop my eyes to my chipped nails, not fully excited about hearing her gush over whatever happened between them.

It's awkwardly silent for a beat, which surprises me, and I glance up, wondering if she realizes how weird it will be for me to hear.

She surprises me by bursting out with laughter. It's her full snort "this is the funniest thing I've ever heard" laugh.

Liam squirms as she wheezes.

I'm having trouble understanding what is funny about my question.

She takes a sip of my water and composes herself.

"We're not together," Maddy explains with such a force that it makes me wonder why she finds the idea so repulsive.

"Why not?" I ask. "You two didn't work out after you…" I can't bring myself to finish that sentence.

"Liam is not Noah's."

I exhale, and I'm sure my relief is visible.

Maddy levels with me. "He may not be the same smug bully when we were younger, but I'm not exactly attracted to a man who only refers to my lady parts in clinical terms." She deepens her voice to mimic his and adds, "'Well, Madeline, it appears you have an incompetent cervix.'"

"Is that a thing?"

She nods. "I went to the free women's clinic four months pregnant and fifteen pounds underweight." Her focus shifts back to Liam, who is happily chewing on a teething ring. "I was...not in a good situation at the time."

My stomach drops. All my problems are champagne problems compared to what she has been through.

I can't believe she let me rant for so long when she clearly has legitimately been through so much shit in her life.

Growing up, her father...well, Maddy stayed with my mom and me as much as she could, and we figured out a few make-up tricks to hide the bruises all over her arms. I hoped she would escape it when she went out on her own, but it's clear that's not the case.

"I'm fine now," she promises, bouncing Liam in her arms. "Really, truly, wonderfully boring and fine."

I'm still stuck on her admission, but she presses on.

"But I bet you can understand my surprise when I sat in a rundown women's clinic wearing one of those disposable thin gowns that doesn't really cover anything, and Noah Washington walked in."

That mental picture makes me cringe. "I would have run out of there as fast as I could."

She kisses Liam's soft head and leans him against her shoulder. "I almost did, but I was so weak and desperate that I just gave in. I'm glad I did. He has been letting Liam and me stay here these past few months." Maddy visibly shivers. "I don't even want to think about the alternative."

"So Liam's father..."

Maddy purses her lips. "Jail," she explains simply. "Life sentence for stabbing an elected official."

I can't believe I complained about something as unimportant as losing out on marketing and promotion support from my label when Maddy had actual problems with grave consequences. I feel about six inches tall.

Liam starts to fuss in her arms. "I'm going to put him down," she says. "I'll be right back. Feel free to raid the fridge or whatever."

She heads toward the room I now assume she shares with Liam.

I wish I had been there for her while she went through everything, but I have the feeling that even if she had my number, she wouldn't have called me. Maddy is notorious for refusing help, especially when it puts a financial strain on someone else, and the fact that she trusts Noah of all people is a complete mind-fuck for me.

In another life, Maddy could pass for a French model. She's all cheekbones and beautiful porcelain skin, and there's something inherently wispy about her. Instead, she got stuck with a dad in a tiny trailer right next to the one my mom rented for us.

It's exceptionally hard to break the low-income cycle, and unfortunately, I claimed the only one-in-a-million chance for this town.

She had dreams of her own, though. Maddy always talked about wanting to be a teacher, and as I went viral and signed with the label, she started taking classes at the community college. Last I spoke to her, she was doing some substitute teaching and after-school tutoring.

What happened to her between then and now, I wonder, touching the baby seat tentatively.

"He's out," Maddy says, practically dancing her way back to me.

We move away from the kitchen and onto a comfortable leather sofa in the living room. It's mostly bare, indicative of Noah's decorating skills, but there are a few baby-related items scattered around this room.

"I still can't believe you're a mom," I admit, tucking my bandaged feet up underneath me.

"And that I live with Noah Washington?"

I laugh. "Yeah, that too."

"He's been great," she says. "I mean it."

I'm not completely ready to believe that yet, so I pry a little more. "I'm surprised he's not living in that mansion with the rest of his family, though. Aren't there multiple *wings* of rooms in that place?"

She frowns.

"What?" I balk. "Is the Gas Grub empire not doing so well?"

She eyes me like I should know that's not possible. Even after all this time, I can still decipher what she is silently saying.

The Washington family's convenience store empire was the front of their business, but it was widely known that they made most of their fortune from less-than-legal sources.

Noah wasn't shy about flaunting his wealth back in school, always making a show of the logos on his wallet and never wearing the same pair of sneakers twice. He once sneered at my glued-together tennis shoes in front of our entire biology class.

And yet, instead of continuing that trend, he seemed to be living a somewhat moderate lifestyle, putting distance between himself and his family. I have the feeling I'm missing a piece of the puzzle that Maddy is about to reveal for me.

"It's not really my place to tell," she starts, but she smiles like she wants to spill it all out.

"Oh come on," I encourage her.

"Okay, you convinced me," she teases. "Remember how Noah was all set to go to Penn State for school?"

I've honestly tried to think as little as possible about him over the years. "I don't, but please continue."

She checks around the room as if Noah is lurking around eavesdropping instead of at work. "His family was on board with it because, at the time, he wanted to study business, which was great for them. Their *empire*. But after a year or so, he changed his mind and switched to medicine without telling anyone. I don't know all of the details, but it didn't come out until after he graduated and was starting medical school. His parents apparently freaked out."

Noah is the only son, and from birth, he was groomed and expected to become part of the family business. The future of it, even. I once referred to him as the next King of Gas Grub.

"Whenever I try to ask him about it, he shuts down, but I don't think he has talked to his family in years," Maddy continues.

"Even his sister?"

She shrugs. "He mentions her every once in a while."

"What about girlfriends? Have they all been okay with you being here?"

"What girlfriends? His work schedule is absolutely insane, not to mention the additional hours he volunteers."

It's too perfect.

There has to be some fault in all of this because it's hard for me to believe that Noah had a complete one-eighty in the time since I left this town.

"Well, I guess he did date Kelsey O'Hadley for a while, but they broke up long before Liam and I came into the picture."

"And there's never been a thing between you two?"

She cocks an eyebrow as if she knows my interest shouldn't be this deep based on what she knows about our history. "No. Absolutely not. Noah did an amazing and helpful thing inviting me to live here. Rent free, I should add. Part of me thinks he did it because he's a little lonely."

"Oh god, Maddy, you feel bad for him," I groan.

"Is that such a bad thing?" Maddy poses.

Maddy, the most warmhearted person I know, has fallen for Noah Washington. Not in the romantic sense...but she has adopted him just like she did me when I moved in next to her.

I'm trying to process it, but I desperately need a subject change. "Kelsey O'Hadley, huh? What has she been up to?" I ask.

Maddy tells me all about how Kelsey got fired from her bank job last year after it came out that she was stealing supplies from the company, then we fall into a nice rhythm of chatting about people we both knew growing up, minus the man whose house we're cozying up in.

She asks me more about Jordan and what our relationship was like, and I indulge her with some happy memories of him and touring life. Maddy is curious about what it's like to live in Los Angeles and points out that my skin is the tannest it has ever been, even with my dedication to SPF.

I dig a little deeper into Liam's father, which she admits was a mistake. Apparently they met through her father, which was more than enough information for me to piece together his character.

My phone buzzes, and I glance at it quickly during the flow of our conversation. It's Adam, texting me new flight details. I avoid it and focus on enjoying more time with Maddy until Liam wakes up and joins the fun.

The three of us have such a nice day together that I'm reluctant to leave, but my mom calls me and asks what she should wear to dinner tonight, reminding me that I need to get back.

Maddy's a little emotional when I leave, but I promise that I will make a point to see her again before I head back to LA. And, of course, I will make sure she always has the right number to call me on.

As I'm driving back to pick my mom up, I make a call to my financial adviser. Maddy and Liam deserve so much more than a life dictated by situations outside their control, and I'm going to help them in a way they cannot refuse.

6

Scott hasn't responded to any of my calls or messages for the past twenty-four hours.

Normally when we're on separate coasts, we can go weeks at a time without catching up, but now that we're a fifteen-minute drive apart, I find it odd that he hasn't gotten in contact with me.

I've been trying to nail down a time that I can see him, and since Adam moved my flight up to tonight, I invite myself over. I'm dreading going back to LA almost as much as I'm dreading telling Scott and my mom that I'm going back to LA.

I sigh and step up to the front door, opening the screen so that I can knock on the metal. My knuckles hit firmly enough that there's no way he would miss the sound. I wait for a beat but hear nothing.

I can't think of a reason why he would ignore me on the phone or in person other than something is very wrong, so I start to panic.

The handle doesn't budge, and for as much time as I've spent here over the years, it just dawns on me now that I don't have a key. I try to see in through the windows, but the curtains are drawn.

I check the most usual places for a spare key, under the welcome mat and under a few potted plants, but come up empty. As I debate on throwing a rock through the window, I see a little stone frog in the garden. I overturn it to find a shiny gold key taped to the bottom.

When the key turns in the lock, I'm hit with darkness and the scent of stale air.

Scott prides himself on keeping a clean home. "Clutter around means clutter inside" is a one-liner I've heard him spout on more than one occasion, so I'm surprised to find everything in a little bit of disarray.

It's not dirty, necessarily, but there are dishes stacked in the sink, worn socks and other laundry scattered on the floor, and a general messiness in the rooms I take in.

"Scott?" I call out.

"In here," he yells back.

Instant relief. "I thought you were dead or something," I say, walking toward his bedroom.

The door is slightly ajar, and I'm thrilled to see the rise and fall of his shoulders. His back is to me as he pulls on a pair of clean socks.

The movement is slow, as if he's in pain, and I rush to his side.

"Oh stop it." He pushes my hands away. "I'm just slow moving this morning. Don't fuss over me. I'm not old yet."

I pointedly look at his hair, which is more gray than brown, and he huffs.

"You didn't answer any of my calls or texts, and I got worried," I admit.

He ignores my concern and walks toward the kitchen. It's the same simple setup it has always been with knick-knacks on the window sill and little magnets on the fridge from the road trips he took with his wife, Beth, before she died from cancer years ago.

I lean against the counter, watching him busy himself with making a pot of coffee.

Something seems off about him, and I can't drop it. "Are you feeling okay?" I press. "Did you get sick after the event or something?"

Once the filter is in, the grounds are set, and the button is switched on, he turns and meets my eyes. Making a big show of it, he picks up his phone and shows no missed calls or messages.

I snatch it from his hand. "You have it on airplane mode," I groan, rolling my eyes.

Scott laughs and shrugs while I show him how to undo it.

"I really thought something was wrong," I say.

"Maybe you think too much," he quips.

I roll my eyes. "Overthinking isn't the worst character trait, and you know it."

The coffee maker beeps, and he pours two cups, adding more milk than coffee to mine, just how I like it.

"Thank you," I say after I take my first sip.

"You hungry?"

I nod. "We can go out if you want."

When I watched him accept his award the other night, I thought his haunted appearance was because of nerves or the lighting, but seeing him again with the morning sun streaming through his window, my concern bubbles up again. He does look a little thinner than usual.

The last thing I want to do is burden him, but he's pulling out all the ingredients to make his sausage gravy from scratch. I can't hide my elation.

"How about I cook and you talk?" Scott suggests. "Fill me in on what's been happening these past few months."

I tell him about a few shows I did in California and how one of Jordan's alleged biggest fans heckled me during a set. A teen drama featured one of my early songs in their special Valentine's Day episode, and I got nearly ten million new streams within that week.

I continue rattling off random little stories about my world, and it guts me to realize that is all I have to share with him.

Every single thing I do revolves around performing, writing, not writing, mixing, distribution, streams, and it's all bullshit. I have no real personal life, other than a few surface-level friends I've made through industry events, unless you count my daily calls and reminders from Adam trying to convince me to write the next greatest album ever —his words, not mine.

Yesterday's vent session with Maddy meant so much to me. Not only did I get to reconnect with an old and true friend but she gave me some much-needed perspective.

I debate about filling in Scott on what's happening with the label, but he views me with such pride, nudging me for more details on every single thing that I feel and experience on stage and at different events. And I can't bear to disappoint him.

He pulls biscuits out of the oven and begins plating the feast. My stomach grumbles in anticipation of all the carbohydrates, and I'm thankful I'm no longer in the land of cold-pressed juices and athleisure clothing. I set the table and top off our cups of coffee.

"Enough about me," I finally say. "Tell me about what's been happening with you. What are your plans for this summer?"

Scott uses the breaks from school in the summer and winter to focus on his own work. Usually he'll write short stories or little poems, but last year he was asked to edit an anthology of non-fiction stories about Pittsburgh. I have an autographed copy back in LA, and it's more precious to me than the awards on that shelf.

"I'm thinking about taking the summer off," he admits.

I shove a heaping bite into my mouth and stop myself from weeping with joy at the taste of the food. The spicy sausage, richness of the gravy, and doughiness of the biscuit I use to soak it all up are so delicious I could honestly cry.

"Off?" I ask, covering my mouth with my hand so I don't have to swallow too fast and give up prematurely on enjoying how good the food is. "To do what?"

"I think it's good every now and again to give yourself a break," Scott says casually.

My eyes narrow at him because I'm sensing an ulterior motive. I doubt that Maddy reached out to him; although, I know they've kept in touch here and there over the years.

"And I think it's time I took one," he continues. "Maybe I'll pick up a new hobby, like painting or software development."

I balk at him. "That sounds like a career change to me."

He shrugs. "Nothing wrong with trying something new."

"Well, maybe you should spend more time cooking," I suggest. "Because I definitely miss eating what you make."

"If you came around more…" Scott teases.

The last thing he wants me to do is stick around. He has made that clear over the years.

He always says I need to be "out there," focusing on my writing and going on adventures. He doesn't know I haven't been doing much of either lately.

We finish up our breakfast, and I'm almost too stuffed to move.

I help him clean up, insisting that I do all the hand washing since he did all the cooking. It also gives me an excuse to tackle the ones sitting in his sink. I wonder if I can somehow hire a cleaning service to come help out around the house without deeply offending him.

I turn to ask him if he can grab another dry towel for the dishes, but when I do, I'm horrified to see Scott swaying in place, gripping the counter to try and remain upright.

The soap bubbles fly as I drop the plate back into the sink with a clunk.

I rush over to Scott for the second time, and now, he doesn't wave me off. He's the palest I've ever seen him. I try to direct him to a chair as his eyes roll in the back of his head and he collapses.

I scream when he hits the floor with a thud.

"Scott? Scott? SCOTT!"

His mouth garbles, a good sign that he's still breathing.

My hands shake as I pull my phone from my pocket and call for help.

The dispatcher speaks in gentle but clear tones, assuring me that help is on the way. I'm hysterical, yet I have a fleeting thought that gossip magazines tend to publicize emergency calls because they're public record. That's another thing I don't need to deal with right now, but I can't get myself together.

Scott's eyes shoot open, scaring the shit out of me, and he takes in his surroundings to piece together what happened to him.

The woman on the phone is asking me a ton of questions, but the one I register is her asking me why I just screamed.

"He's awake," I whisper.

"Don't let him move," she demands. "Not until the paramedics arrive."

I place my hands on the side of his face and encourage him to stay still. His eyes are wide, and his skin is clammy. He's acting like a really drunk person trying to prove they're sober, mouthing that he is fine, but I don't let go.

It feels like hour, instead of minutes, until the paramedics are at the door, rolling in a cart to take him out. They ask him and me questions, and I answer as best I can.

I grab my purse and Scott's wallet from the counter before I slide into the back of the ambulance with them.

"We'll have you over to Passavant Hospital in fifteen minutes, Scott," one of the paramedics tells him. "Can you focus on breathing deeply until we get you there?"

"Allegheny General," Scott insists, pulling at his oxygen mask.

The paramedic shrugs and tells the other the change of plans. "You have a doctor there?"

Scott nods. "Dr. Prewett."

I don't miss the flicker of pity across the paramedic's face, but I tuck that away because Scott reaches for my hand.

"It's going to be fine," Scott reassures me.

I feel like it should really be the other way around. He shouldn't be the one doling out reassurance in this situation, but the tears pool in my eyes, so I squeeze his hand even tighter.

Sound ceases to exist around me as we speed toward the hospital.

We bypass the emergency room and are admitted straight to a private room on the third floor, which seems odd but I don't question it. If it's special treatment because it's me, it's probably the only time I don't actually care; I only want Scott to be okay.

The next few hours are slow and frustrating.

A few nurses and at least two doctors come in the room, taking his vitals and asking questions but giving no answers. Someone comes back to draw blood, and I get a little squeamish at the sight of it, which makes Scott chuckle.

Another hospital employee brings lunch on a tray for him, and he picks at it, insisting he is still full from breakfast. He offers it to me, and I decline. Jell-O has always weirded me out.

Scott sleeps on and off, and I don't bother to turn on the television, finding the sounds of the machines working and noise from the hallway comforting interruptions amid the silence.

Every single time he shifts or makes the slightest noise, my body goes rigid, preparing for him to faint again, and he scolds me, reminding me that he's not made of glass.

"It was just a little fainting spell," he says nonchalantly.

"A little fainting spell?" My voice is high and incredulous. "You passed out, fell over, and hit your head on the floor while your tongue waggled and your eyes rolled back. Don't be so dismissive of this. You could have a concussion or a deficiency or something."

Guilt flashes across his features, and just as I open my mouth to question it, Noah walks in.

I do a double take.

Noah fucking Washington.

In those too-tight scrubs that cling to his chest.

"Mr. Davis," Noah says brightly. "You might not remember me, but I'm—"

"Noah Washington," Scott interrupts. "Of course I remember you."

Why does he keep doing that? Does he really expect himself to be forgettable? I have to stop myself from saying those exact words to him.

Noah nods and strides over to the side of the bed. He's completely focused on Scott, asking him how he is feeling now compared to this morning and if he's in any pain. Thankfully, Scott says he is feeling better, stronger even.

"Dr. Prewett is on vacation, so I'm going—"

"I thought you were a gynecologist," I snap at Noah.

He eyes me for the first time, and I refuse to falter under the intensity of his glare.

"I was volunteering in the women's clinic when I met

Maddy, if that's what you're trying to get at," he says evenly.

I press my lips together. Of course, newly minted savior Noah has to volunteer to help battered and poor women in his spare time. I pause, realizing I'm bitter about someone helping people, and wonder if I really am the shittier person out of the two of us.

"I'm in my final year of residency here," Noah tells Scott. "This isn't my current rotation, but I asked if I could step in when the nurse pulled your file. Are you okay with this, Mr. Davis?"

I haven't filled him in on the last two encounters with Noah, but Scott knows enough about my history with Noah to understand that this is complicated. He eyes me to make sure that I'm okay with this, and I squeeze his hand in response, a silent confirmation that it's okay.

Noah's a medical professional, after all, even if he is an asshole.

"Fine with me," Scott says. "But 'Scott' is fine. I haven't been your teacher for a long time."

Noah nods. "Good. I never did my reading for 'Great Expectations' anyway."

That makes Scott snort.

"So why don't we start out with you filling me in on what happened earlier today."

"We've already told three other people what happened," I groan. "Don't you guys share notes?"

Noah has the nerve to smile at me. "We do, but I like to hear it directly from the patient myself."

His patience unnerves me. Once again, he is collected and in control of himself, while I'm a frazzled and wrinkled mess. We've barely spoken to each other and yet he's completely under my skin.

I sink back in the chair and let them continue.

"We just finished breakfast," Scott says, patient as can be even though this is the fourth time he is retelling it. "I was standing in the kitchen, and all of a sudden I felt weak and then nothing, and the next thing I know, I'm awake with this one," he points to me, "holding my face until I'm whisked away in an ambulance."

Noah turns to me. "Anything unusual about the fall?"

"I don't think so, but I'm not sure how hard he hit his head."

"Have you been eating regularly?" Noah asks him.

"Not as much as I used to," he admits.

"Your temperature is normal, that's good. I see some bruises forming on your elbows. Anywhere else that's happening?"

Scott glances downward. "On my legs a bit."

Noah nods. "Nothing seems amiss to me given the progression and the notes from your appointment with Dr. Prewett in May. I'm sure he'll want to see you next week when he's back in the office since this is the third time you've fainted in the past few months, but for now, let's get you up for a CT to check on that head, and we'll hold you overnight for observation just to be safe."

Third time?

I'm seething. "What is he talking about, Scott? This has happened before?"

Scott shoots Noah a "Thanks so much, buddy" look.

"What is going on here?" I demand. "What aren't you telling me?"

I glance at Noah, knowing he is useless and can't tell me because of doctor-patient confidentiality. Noah busies himself with Scott's chart, refusing to meet my eyes. Of course, now that I want him to actually pay attention to me, he spaces out.

Scott looks at me as if he's preparing to shatter my heart in a million pieces, and then he does with four words. "I have cancer, kiddo."

7

I have cancer, kiddo.

I heard what he said, but I'm focusing on what he didn't say. The words weren't "I'm fighting cancer" or "I'm kicking cancer's ass." No. It was as if he was admitting defeat to me, and I don't know how to rationalize that.

He repeats the words once again, then presses on, watching my frozen form as he speaks. "I found out right before Christmas."

Christmas. A three-day trip because it fell over a weekend and it was a good pit stop on the way to my performance in New York. It was fine, just like every other Christmas, except Scott found out he was dying days before then and didn't say anything about it.

"I didn't want to tell you because you had that big performance on New Year's Eve," Scott admits. "Then it just felt weird to tell you over the phone."

I chew on my bottom lip as the hot tears roll down my

cheeks. I don't bother to wipe them because more just keep falling, and I can't keep up.

"It was never the right time."

Had I not come back for the awards ceremony, would he have never told me? Would my mom or his lawyer have called me one day out of the blue to tell me that Scott was dead and I had to come back so we could put him in the ground?

The urge to scream at him tugs at my psyche, but that is probably the last thing he needs right now. I want to be a strong fixture by his side, not someone he has to coddle while he fights for his life.

I swallow. "What kind of cancer is it?" My voice is barely above a whisper.

Scott looks at Noah and encourages him with a wave. "I'll let the doctor here do his thing."

Noah sits down in the chair on the other side of the hospital bed. It's like we're sitting across from each other ready to negotiate, but instead of an expensive wood table, Scott is there as a barrier.

He begins to explain what's happening, even showing me x-rays and the results of testing and bloodwork.

I try to keep up, but he's using a lot of technical terms. I wonder if it's partly to make me feel stupid. I shake off the unnecessary resentment and pick up "leukemia" and "declined chemotherapy."

"You're not getting treatment for this?" I screech to Scott, completely abandoning my calm, supportive persona.

Honestly, it was only a matter of time.

Noah excuses himself, giving us the space and privacy to talk it out.

"Why aren't you fighting this, Scott?" I ask.

Scott swallows and grabs my hand, willing me to hear what he is going to say. "Beth."

His wife.

Over the years, I've learned a little about her, but he never goes into too much detail about the last two years they had together. She had an aggressive form of breast cancer, and by the time it was found, it spread all over. He begged her to do chemo, to do all the experimental drugs and trials, and she went along with it.

I saw a picture of her once from that time, and she looked like a skeleton. A beautiful one, of course, but she was run ragged and didn't get to enjoy her last days on the earth because she just dove into one fight after another until her heart gave out.

Fifteen years of being with someone every single day, and it ends.

Scott watches me consider this.

"But that was a long time ago, Scott, and I'm sure things are different and better now. I always see news articles about experimental trials and breakthroughs—"

"I'm not changing my mind, Liv," he says firmly.

It's his teacher voice, and it's been a long time since I've heard it.

Despite this day and everything I learned in the past ten minutes, it makes me want to smile.

I don't, though. I merely wipe the tears away from my face and nod.

Scott's as stubborn as he is everything else, and if it's already been this long, I doubt there is anything I can do to change things. It might even be too late to recover.

I know this, but it doesn't mean I don't want to get on my knees and beg. That would be selfish of me, though, to ask him to prolong his pain and suffering on my behalf, just like it's selfish of him to ask me to let him go.

We hold hands until a woman who identifies herself as "Jeanine from radiology" comes by to wheel Scott up for his CT scan. He refuses the wheelchair at first, so I have to remind him he has already won a tremendous battle today and it's best not to push his luck.

When he is gone, I release my composure.

The tears fall again, but this time, a deep, sobbing inhale comes along with it. I let it all out for a few minutes and prepare for the worst scenario possible of losing him— and soon. I blow my nose with a wad of tissues and hiccup, and I'm disgusted with myself and this reality.

Everything has turned to shit since I've arrived back in Hell, as usual.

Without him, the room feels small, and I want out. I wash my hands and rinse my face in the ensuite before I make a hasty exit. My face is already blotchy and swollen from all the emotion, and I hope it goes down before Scott comes back. If he has limited time left on earth, I don't need one of his last memories to be my ugly crying face.

In the panic, I forgot my hat and sunglasses, but I keep my head down and no one stops me or flashes any recognition as I wind through the halls. I figure I have about an hour to get my shit back together, and I think going outside will help.

I find a vacant bench at the edge of the parking lot.

As uncomfortable as the wooden slats are, I'm happy to

breathe in the fresh air instead of the harsh scent of industrial cleaner. I focus on my breathing, somewhat relieved to find I have control over my tears.

The buzzing of my phone distracts me from the attempt at meditation, and I sigh at Adam's name and picture. I ignore it and see that I have five other missed calls from him and a slew of text messages.

Nothing urgent, other than my career hanging in the balance and the fact that my flight to Los Angeles boards in an hour.

I don't have the mental capacity to deal with any of that shit right now. The sun on my skin feels divine, so that's what I focus my attention on. I'm actually working my mind back to a normal place when I feel someone slide onto the bench next to me.

Before I even open my eyes, I pick up on a woodsy scent, and I know it's Noah.

Noah fucking Washington.

"You okay?"

I really need him to stop asking me that question, but I'm not in the mood to verbally spar with him right now.

"Yeah," I sigh, and it's all I can muster as a response.

I close my eyes again and tilt my face up toward the sun, but I'm distracted by his presence.

Somehow, we're closer in proximity than we were in his car, and I'm incredibly conscious of it. It doesn't help that instead of the summer air, I keep breathing in his aftershave or deodorant or whatever smells so damn good.

I do my best to catalog it in my mind and wonder if I should try and find it at the store so I can spray it on my pillow at night or rub it all over my skin after I shower. I try not to think about Noah toweling off, staring at himself in the mirror as he drops his towel and—

My phone buzzes again.

I press the side button so it'll eventually go to voice-mail, and I'm guessing Noah watched the motion because the next thing I know, he's shifting, rattling the entire bench and asking, "Do you want me to call someone for you?"

"No," I say while shaking my head.

He thinks that it's someone who gives a shit about me. Someone concerned about my location or well-being, but it's just my manager trying to coerce me back across the country to get my ass handed to me in a conference room.

I swallow, and I swear it's the loudest sound I've ever heard.

A new wave of tears threatens as I realize how alone I am in this grief, how responsible I feel to push along the memory of Scott, someone who has been a life-changing influence for me but whose legacy won't extend too far past his lifetime.

Noah starts to ask me another question, but I cut him off, finally opening my eyes to stare at him directly.

"Noah," I plead. "If you're going to sit here, can you at least shut the fuck up?"

A smile threatens to surface on his face, but he pushes it away.

He leans back, mimicking my posture, and it's not lost on me that I'm somehow being comforted without actually being comforted by Noah Washington, of all people.

Instead of replaying the greatest hits version of him

torturing me in high school like I have been doing in his presence, I just sit. In complete silence. With my mind focusing on absolutely nothing except the sound of the main doors opening in the distance and the cars coming and going around us.

We stay like that until he glances at his beeper and tells me that Scott is heading back to his room.

I stand and stretch upward, and I'm conscious that Noah impatiently watches the movement.

He has sat out here with me for the past thirty minutes, yet somehow, taking another ten seconds of his precious time is too much for him? I didn't even ask him to or expect him to offer this weird show of compassion.

It continues, however, as he leads me through the employee entrance and restricted sections of the hospital back to the right room. He leaves before I can thank him.

When Scott comes back, he has a tentative expression, as if he has no idea what state I'll be in when he returns. He seems pleased that I am collected, although a little more puffy than usual.

Somewhere between the CT scan and the hospital room, Scott got his hands on today's paper. He reads it while I stare off into space, still ignoring Adam's phone calls.

"You know," Scott says. "Noah's in pediatrics."

"I didn't know." My voice is dull, so I try to bring it back up a few notches to normalcy and keep a conversation going. "Who told you that?" I ask.

He shrugs. "Jeanine from radiology told me as she wheeled me all around. Kept gushing about how great he is with patients and how the kids and their parents all love him."

Of course they love him and his selfless savior persona he has now taken on.

"Did you tell her what an absolute fucking dickwad he was in high school?" I deadpan.

Scott breaks out into laughter. "Do I even want to know what a dickwad is?"

I didn't consider what the literal term was, and it does make me chuckle a little bit, especially with his deep roar of laughter egging me on. We settle down after a few minutes, and I go back to watching him read the paper while the Jell-O melts into a weird puddle.

The sadness threatens to creep in again as I start to wonder how many other moments like this we'll have, enjoying the stillness and comfort of each other's presence.

Scott always says that the sign of a true friend is one you can sit in complete silence with and not feel any obligation to fill it with meaningless words.

If that's true, what does that make Noah and me? Friends? I scoff at the idea.

Scott, however, is more than a friend—he's like a father figure for me. He's been more than a teacher and a mentor for a long time. Even though we don't see each other every single day, there's something reassuring about the fact that I get to see him on holidays and call him whenever.

Well, I guess there's a limit on "whenever" now.

"How long do we have?" I ask quietly, and I dread the answer.

Scott coughs, clearing out his throat. "At Christmas, it

was a year, in March everything was moving quickly, down to six months, and now, who knows."

"That's not even…" I stop.

"Don't include me in your Thanksgiving plans," he says lightly.

I frown. "But you promised you'd come to New York for New Year's Eve this year if I got booked again," I remind him, as if that's going to change anything.

"I'll see what I can do," he says and goes back to the arts and leisure section.

I pick up my phone. Adam's chat bubble indicates he is typing his seven millionth text to me, this latest stream about how he knows I'm not checked in or on the plane headed back.

For the first time ever, I'm about to stand up to the label and his decision. I've let them push me around about tour dates and lyric changes and so many other things, but this is non-negotiable.

My fingers fly. *I'm done.*

WHAT??????????

I roll my eyes. As if Adam didn't see this coming.

Tell them to release me. I'm not coming back, and I don't have anything done. I'm not going to do it.

The image of him sweating in his eight-hundred-dollar suit lightens my mood a fraction.

Scott senses the change, smiles, and pats my knee. If he had any idea what I was doing from a foot away from him, I imagine his reaction would be quite different.

Adam floods our chat with a barrage of all caps messages asking me if I am sane, telling me I'm killing my career, begging me to pick up the phone and call him before I do something I'm going to regret.

As a response, I open up the social media platform with my biggest following. Ignoring the red notifications of people liking and commenting and messaging me, I double-check my settings to make sure my phone won't get over-loaded once I'm finished typing this message.

I'm practically convulsing with joy at the idea of this, but I'm righted again when I glance over at the hospital bed, and the pit in my stomach comes back. I'm not even self-editing my post, which is probably the worst thing I can do as a writer, but I need to get this out without a second of hesitation.

Hello all. It's me (obviously).

I know that you have been promised a new album this year, but I'm sad to say, it's not happening. These past ten years with you have been everything I could have ever dreamed of but I need to take a hiatus for—

I glance up at Scott again.

—the rest of the year. I'm so grateful for all of your love and support. Seriously, you all have been amazing. I promise to be back next year, but for now, I need to focus on family and healing.

I love you all. And thank you again.

It's a little coy, a little melodramatic, but I post it.

Almost immediately, the speculations come in through the comments that I'm in rehab or broken up about some vacation Jordan and his girlfriend just took. I set the phone down and watch the notifications come in from the app, calls from my manager, texts from Jordan, even, and a few west coast acquaintances.

It's like watching a movie of someone else's life unfold,

and it stuns me how disconnected I feel from it. I turn off my phone and toss it into my bag.

"What did you do?" Scott asks, taking in whatever emotions I'm revealing on my face.

He's sick, not totally unaware, I remind myself.

I shrug and mumble that I'm going to go track down some coffee. I get lost on multiple floors and elevators until I make my way to the pediatrics floor, where Noah leans on a counter and talks to a nurse.

It's precisely the image I had conjured up at the idea of him being a doctor and hitting on nurses and patients, but when I look closer, I realize how serious his expression is, even more so than usual, and he looks ragged as hell.

He sees me approach and readies himself for whatever abuse I'm going to unleash on him.

"Noah, I need your help," I say, swallowing my pride.

The nurse's eyebrows shoot up, likely because I don't call him *Dr. Washington* and fawn all over him.

"Okay," he says. "What is it?"

I stare at him for a moment, trying to see him as the man Maddy sees, the one who disappointed his family by choosing a career path to help people. It's difficult to wrap my mind around it, but Scott's needs should be my only priority right now.

"Can you tell me everything?" I ask. "In normal human terms, not doctor ones. I just...need to understand what we're up against...what he can and cannot do and how this...ends."

I can't help but hate myself for how desperate and broken I sound, but it's *Scott*.

Noah and I are toe to toe, and I nearly crumple as he stares at me.

I remind myself that he's a doctor, and this is his job. He swore an oath and everything.

Still, it takes him a minute to soften and start explaining.

8

The nurse apologizes about a dozen times when she comes to tell me that visiting hours are up. I promise Scott I'll be back the next day before I head out, and it's more difficult to leave him than I thought.

From now on, every single time I say goodbye, it could be the last time.

I'm pleased to find there are a few taxis waiting outside the hospital. I ask one to take me to Scott's house, and I finally turn my phone back on to call Adam when I buckle my seatbelt.

He is having a full level-ten meltdown, and I let him rant. He screams through the phone for the entire ride back, and he continues as I start packings some Scott's things, including his collection of favorite poetry books.

It feels weird to be going through his drawers, folding up a bunch of his clothes, and packing his toiletries up for him, like I'm invading his privacy. In a way, I am. There's no way he's living here alone while I'm in town.

He made the decision not to tell me about what was happening, and I refuse to give him the opportunity to hurt himself again.

I lug two suitcases and a plastic bin I found in one of his closets into my car, deciding I'll send someone else to clean out the fridge and do a deep clean of the house later. I take down a few pictures from his wall of him and Beth and a few other little trinkets in the house.

I just have to decide where everything goes in my house, but it all has to be ready by the time Scott is discharged tomorrow.

My phone is warm on my leg from use when I pull into my own garage and turn off the car.

I try to interrupt Adam's continued yelling, but I'm not successful. When I hang up on him, he immediately calls me back, so I go back to ignoring him.

The most logical thing to do is to put Scott up in one of the already done guest rooms, but based on what Noah said, going up and down the stairs might eventually be a challenge.

I lug Scott's stuff over to the office and fling open the double doors. It's the darkest room in the house and the most masculine, and it's rarely used.

The wood paneled walls and soft gray carpet will do, I decide, but the office furniture will have to be moved down into that creepy storage area of the basement that I refuse to go into. It's also right next to my rarely used home studio. This basement alone is bigger than my condo in LA, and I don't even use it.

Normally, I would call Adam and ask one of his many assistants to arrange movers and a furniture delivery, but that is definitely not an option right now, so I spend twenty minutes on the phone and cough up my credit card number to make it all happen as soon as possible.

As I'm walking back to the kitchen, poorer but self-sufficient, my mom tears down the stairs.

It's the fastest I've ever seen her move, and she's in complete disarray. Her mousy brown hair is wrapped up in a towel. She usually insists on being immaculately presented at all times, even in our own home.

She appears to be fueled by rage. "What the hell is this?" she asks, holding up her phone to show me my own post.

I squint, noting that it now has more than one million likes. I'm glad I turned off the notifications while I was in the hospital or my phone would explode from all the buzzing and alerts.

"Oh that," I say, and I know it's calm enough to infuriate her. "Well, it's just—"

My mother doesn't even give me time to explain. "Adam called me in a complete panic," she starts.

She rips the towel off her head and twists the fabric in frustration.

I probably should have given her some warning about what was happening with the label or with Scott in the hospital, and I'm a little ashamed to say that it didn't occur to me to do either.

Our communication is usually strictly around the holidays or the rare times I am home visiting, but she is the only person from my hometown who has made the trip to see me on the west coast. I've offered to move her out with me, but she prefers the smaller town life she has created for herself here.

The more she speaks, the more wound up she gets. "He's so worried about you, saying all of this nonsense about how you're in a dispute with the label and they're threatening to drop you."

"Mom," I interject, but she presses on.

"And of course, I can't get in touch with you because you're with Scott and you're declining my calls."

I pinch the bridge of my nose. "My phone was off," I say by way of explanation.

Happily declining work-related calls is one thing, but I would never purposely ignore my own mother.

"Because why would you answer me when you have Scott? You're here for a week, and you've already spent more time with him than you have your own mother."

"That's not true."

Everything I say falls on deaf ears, so for the second time today, I let someone who cares more about how my faltering career is going to impact them rant to me about it. Unlike Adam, who has never met Scott, the history between my mother and my mentor is a little contentious.

I didn't realize it until my sophomore year of high school when I brought home an official letter with the news that I won a local writing contest. She was excited for me but kept questioning Scott's involvement, trying to suss out how much influence he had over me.

It has always confused me, given their very limited in-person interactions, but I didn't press the issue.

From then on, whenever I would spend time with him or mention that he was helping me or that he had an idea of something I could work on, she'd get weirdly territorial about spending time with me.

This trip started off on the wrong foot because the travel hell meant I missed dinner with her before Scott's award presentation. I tried to make it up to her by spending at least two meals with her instead of rushing over to his house, but judging by her reaction, it wasn't enough.

If I hadn't been there this morning...I swallow and shake off the vision of him passing out on his kitchen floor.

"You're unbelievable, Liv. This is just like high school all over—"

My vision turns red, and I have no patience for this any longer. "Scott is dying," I cry.

She pauses finally. I watch her swallow her words with wide eyes.

Perhaps I could have been more tactful, but at least it's out in the open now.

Her entire self-righteous demeanor crumples, and her voice is shaky when she speaks. "What did you say?"

"I was over at his house this morning for breakfast, and he fainted," I begin to explain.

Finally having her undivided attention, I fill her in on the rest, like how he has been having these spells because of his cancer and how he is deteriorating rapidly.

She's quiet when I finish, digesting all of the new horrible information I presented. I'm surprised to see the redness around her eyes as she holds back tears.

I move to pull her into a hug, but she balks, as if she's too delicate in her processing to be disturbed. I nod, giving her space.

As I walk back down the hall, I finally allow myself to

accept the emptiness inside. I contemplate the new normal of being here in Pennsylvania indefinitely, with no career path ahead of me and my heart breaking for a man who has been like a father to me.

I feel like a stranger in my own home. My eyes glaze over all of the white furniture, cabinets, and walls. The brown wood floors contrast the sterileness, and I honestly can't remember if my mother purposely decorated the house to be a blank sheet of nothing or if it was like that when I bought it.

My feet are cement blocks as I drag myself up the stairs.

It's sad how exhausted I am, and I can't withhold the groan that escapes my lips as I walk. My bedroom is at the opposite end of the hall from the master suite where my mother took up residency. It's odd that she claimed it, given that this is *my* house, but just like the decor, I merely shrug it off.

I'm pathetic, but at least I own up to it.

I remember the night Maddy and I first saw this house. We became licensed drivers at sixteen-and-a-half, and when we had enough gas in the tank to do so, we drove all over town. We cruised all around different neighborhoods to check out the houses, being "nebby," as we say in Pittsburgh. On one particularly beautiful summer night, we saw it.

We both stared, lost in the beauty of the exterior and the lighting. It was as close to a castle as I'd ever seen in person, and I imagined myself living in it someday.

At the time, it was a pipe dream, considering that my mom and I constantly bumped elbows in our one-bedroom trailer. I never thought I'd escape Pennsylvania, let alone travel the world. But here I am.

I head straight for the large soaker tub in the bathroom attached to my bedroom, pouring in a generous amount of bubbles before I tear off my clothes and sink in once the water is high enough.

My enjoyment is palpable, and the heat is doing wonderful things to fight the rigidness of my limbs. I feel a little guilty, thinking of Scott alone in his hospital bed while I'm here floating and breathing in the scent of lavender.

I shake off the mental picture of my mentor. I don't want to think of anything at all right now. I close my eyes and submerge as much of myself as I can, dragging my fingers through the bubbles.

I'm the first one at school.

We're supposed to arrive early today for the field trip, but I'm extra early because my mom had to open the salon today.

I'm by myself, which I don't mind in any setting except for school, where loneliness is a vulnerability. I wish Maddy's dad would have signed the permission slip or she would have let me forge it for her, but she was too afraid he would find out.

"You're such a goddamn disappointment."

I peek around the corner of the building. I hold in a gasp when I see Noah and his father, staring at each other over the roof of his dad's car, doors ajar.

Noah looks so much like his father. It's scary, really, how dark and dangerous they both look yet somehow so beautiful. Noah's dad is in an expensive tailored suit, and Noah's designer outfit probably cost more than my mom's car. I frown at my beat-up Converse, well-worn skirt, and blue top from the discount rack at Target.

"You think I care about some stupid field trip, Noah? I have a fucking empire to run, and someday you will, too."

"Maybe I won't."

"What did you say?" Noah's father's simmering anger is now full-on boiling.

Noah doesn't respond, though, and it only infuriates his father more, causing him to storm to the other side of the car and shove him up against the side of it.

"What did you just fucking say to me?"

They're so close.

If anything, I admire Noah's strong chin and ability to not break down. I would have come undone if someone was that angry at me and that close to my face.

Then again, I was powerless and poor.

Noah had it all.

Or so I thought.

"You ungrateful little piece of shit."

Despite everything Noah has done to me, my gut instinct is to help him before it gets too out of hand, so I stand up, brush off my skirt, and turn the corner.

"Noah!" I say as excitedly as I can.

They both freeze.

"I thought I heard you. My mom had to drop me off early, too, and I was wondering if you wanted to wait together. I have a question about the history homework I wanted to ask for your help on," I ramble, and I'm regretting my actions in real-time as they happen.

Noah's father's face is a polite, cool expression instantly, which is as terrifying as it is fascinating, but Noah's eyes narrow in my direction, as if he's angry at me for jumping to help him.

His father releases the front of his shirt and pats him twice on the cheek, not gently, before he gets in the car.

Noah slams the door, tosses his backpack over his shoulder, and strides by me without another word.

"Noah," I call after him, but he doesn't turn around.

I don't see him again until we're on the bus. I'm sitting alone up front, but I look back over my shoulder. He's surrounded by friends who are all laughing and messing around while we're speeding down the highway.

He keeps up with those around him, but there's something vacant in his expression that I can't really explain. His eyes narrow when they meet my gaze, and I immediately turn around, feeling the burning of his scrutiny on me for the rest of the afternoon.

I saw a side of him that no one else sees.

Growing up, there were rumors of violence and cruelty in the Washington family, starting from the top with his grandfather, a disgraced senator who was removed from office after it came out that he was using his political power to influence his own businesses.

As it usually went with corruption, the rumor was that their wealth only grew even more once he was out of office and out of the courtrooms without a mark on his record.

In the many times Noah and his family got photographed at events and ground-breaking ceremonies, they all stood beside one another, dressed immaculately and noticeably stiff.

Even at our high school graduation, when Maddy and I posed back to back while my mom took pictures on her second-hand digital camera, I caught a glimpse of Noah with his family. They stood together with their noses turned up, waiting for the moment they could leave. His sister, who was about five years younger than us, stood with a sneer on her face.

I frown. A loveless childhood isn't an excuse to project his frustration onto other people, to bully them relentlessly in the hallways at school, but I reflect on my own way of thinking. I was so influenced by everyone around me, so concerned with how I was perceived, and I had no pressure at home to do so.

Noah, however, was born to take over the Washington family businesses. He was groomed to continue the tradition of skirting the rules, to believe that other people were lesser than him because they needed help to survive. They wanted him to uphold their skewed values.

I'm finding empathy for the person I've despised since high school, and I'm wondering what took me so long to figure it out—and why I'm so relieved that I've found a way to let myself think about Noah without trepidation.

As much as I want to hold onto hating him for reasons I need many hours of therapy to unpack, I have to admit that he has to have changed. His house guests, career choices, and modest living are indicative of a changed man, even if he still treats me with a degree of sharpness.

I step out of the room-temperature water and wrap myself in a soft white towel. Sitting on the edge of the tub, I realize that I just might understand him a little better.

I don't like that I find comfort in that realization.

9

I expect Scott to give me tremendous pushback when I pitch the idea of him coming to live at the house with me and my mother.

He's always been fiercely independent, and I think it's one of the traits he passed on to me—if it's possible to pass on traits without being genetically related, that is.

Sitting beside him as we wait on the final discharge paperwork, I inhale and prepare for a battle. "Scott, I wanted to talk to you about something," I start, nervously tapping my feet as I do so.

He doesn't even bother to put down the newspaper. "If this is about your big dramatic note on *social media*," he says with slight irritation, "I'm already aware of it."

"But you're not on social media," I sputter.

"Oh I'm aware, but it appears all the nurses are," he huffs. "They've been babbling about it since the moment you posted it."

I guess I underestimated the gossip circle of a few hours

alone with nurses, and the absolute last thing Scott wants to be is responsible for my career on a hiatus. I might as well press on with my idea while he's already in a mood.

"Well, that's just a part of it," I admit. "I was going to talk to you about coming to stay with me, and my mom, at the house."

This gets him to put down the paper and glare at me.

"You were the one who was saying all that stuff about how it's good every now and again to take a break," I remind him. "We could do it together. It could be...fun!"

He presses his lips together, scrunching up his entire face. I can't decide if he's angry enough to yell or about to burst out laughing.

A moment passes, and he does neither. He simply picks up his paper and mutters to himself.

"What was that?" I ask.

"Fine," he exhales. "Twist my arm to live in that giant house, I guess."

I laugh. "I already got some of your stuff moved in."

"Pretty presumptuous, don't you think?" Scott says.

He keeps bantering with me as he gets officially discharged, and he almost throws a fit when the nurse, once again, insists he needs a wheelchair to get to my car.

"It's hospital policy," she insists.

By the time we make it home, things are feeling slightly back to normal, except for the fact that I've forced a fifty-year-old man to be my new roommate. Just me, my mother, and my high school English teacher living the dream life. I roll my eyes at my inner monologue.

I lead him inside, and he whistles as he takes in the interior.

I think he has been here once, very briefly to pick me up, since I bought it. He hasn't spent significant time in my own house, despite that I've considered him a key part of what I think of "home," but I guess I always go to his house or go out when I come back to visit.

"I'll give you the tour later," I promise.

"Seems pretty self-explanatory to me," he says, pointing in various directions. "Kitchen, outside, hallway, living room, shitter—"

I fake a gasp. "Language, Scott! For someone who spent his career educating the vulnerable minds of children, I am shocked by your foul mouth."

"I'm on a break," he reminds me. "I won't even use my teacher voice."

"I'll believe that when I don't hear it," I tell him.

I open the double doors of the office, glad that all the furniture arrived this morning as promised.

I didn't end up having the movers take anything to the basement area. I rearranged the room a bit, figuring that Scott might actually like to have a desk to sit and write at. He smiles at the way I've arranged his books.

He eyes the price tag on the massive bed, and I rip it off before he can scold me for the amount.

"I don't know why you made such a big fuss," he says, shaking his head. "I'll be gone by fall."

I can't tell if his lightheartedness is a defense mechanism or if he is really at peace with everything, but either way, I don't fall for it.

"You promised me you'd make it to New Year's Eve," I remind him.

He sits down on the edge of the bed, looking tired from the journey. "I'll see what I can do."

"Do you need anything?"

Before he can yell at me for worrying about him too much, my mom rushes in.

I haven't seen her since the scene in the kitchen yesterday, but I did text her to let her know about the movers and our new roommate. She didn't respond.

"Scott," she exhales.

"Hello, Denise," he says with a smile. "Thank you for having me into your home."

"It wasn't my idea," she explains, shifting awkwardly on her feet. "It's not even technically my house."

"Oh stop, Mom," I huff.

"How nice of her to let you stay here, then," Scott says. "Glad I'm not the only one..."

They turn on me, continuing to make jokes at my expense, and I step back to watch them interact and form a strange camaraderie around it. It's tentative, like they're afraid to step too close, but they're clearly both trying to be as polite as possible toward the other.

I slowly back out of the room and move to start on lunch.

I'm elbows deep in the refrigerator, sorting through the available ingredients, when the doorbell rings.

"Got it," my mom calls eagerly.

I assume it's the nurse I hired to come by every day. I can hear the sounds of chatter leading to Scott's room, so I continue on.

My cooking abilities are very limited. I spend a fair amount of time flipping between the refrigerator, freezer, and pantry trying to figure out what I can pull together, and nothing jumps out at me immediately.

If Scott's serious about learning a new thing or two, maybe I can find my inner chef. Yep, I can see it. Really owning the kitchen. I visualize myself whipping up amazing meals and plating them beautifully and being one of those people who creates art with their hands.

I laugh at myself and shake off that thought. I already have an art. No matter how romantic or idyllic making a soufflé or creating a clay pot with one of those spinning machines seems, I don't need to go around stealing creative space from other people.

Instead, I just enjoy the motion. I decide on a stir fry, which isn't that easy to mess up, even if I get lost in the process of it. Chopping vegetables is therapeutic, and I love the smell of garlic and soy sauce mixed together.

While everything sizzles in the pan, I hum a New Order song that's been stuck in my head since I heard it on the way to the hospital. I stir occasionally, but I'm trying to remember the words to the fourth verse. It's driving me crazy that I can't recall them.

Once I look it up on my phone, I close my eyes and sing softly.

I don't come back to earth again until I hear a noise in the hallway. I turn the burner to low and put a lid over the pan to keep everything warm.

I wipe my hands on a towel, and as I walk toward the den, I'm stopped in my tracks by Noah.

Noah fucking Washington.

In my house.

Listening to me sing.

And staring at framed pictures of me in the hallway.

I don't know which one of these mortifies me the most, but he seems generally unfazed.

"What are you doing here?" I ask.

The answer is obvious. He came here with the nurse to check on Scott, which is equal parts endearing and over-bearing.

He ignores me, keeping his focus on what's in front of him.

I watch him take in the pictures, and then I turn to the wall myself, trying to see what he is seeing.

I roll my eyes at the picture of my wedding day. Jordan and I eloped, telling no one until after the fact.

My mom met him during our first Christmas together and loved him immediately, showing him more care and tenderness than I received my entire life. Scott warmed up to him eventually. I didn't press the relationship, not wanting to force something that wasn't there.

When we split, my mother was heartbroken.

Scott just shrugged while taking a sip of coffee and said, "At least you don't have to pretend to like basketball anymore." I laughed until I cried.

Looking back at the wall now, I force my gaze away from the happy faces on myself and my ex-husband. There are a few pictures of me over the years, performing at different venues and others from when I was a baby, but Noah stares at a picture of Maddy and me.

It's one of my favorites. It was one of the few moments of bliss during the teenage years. Maddy had just gotten a digital camera for her eighteenth birthday on July Fourth, a much-needed upgrade from my mom's old one we used.

Usually, we stayed in, binged on snacks, and watched fireworks and whatever was on MTV, but that year, we went to a party some of the theatre kids threw. She insisted on documenting all of it.

We figured out how to use the self-timer, and she propped her camera up and dove toward me on the grass before it ran out. In the photo, we're in hysterics, and her hair is nearly vertical as her knee drives into my pelvis.

Life was simpler before every phone had a camera on it and everyone filtered themselves into perfection.

Noah looks at me, jarring me out of my memories. "I'm just checking in."

His face is so serene, and I wonder if he is comparing notes to his own childhood.

"What?" I ask.

"I wanted to check on Scott and make sure the transition out of the hospital was smooth."

I blink, remembering the reason why he is standing here in the first place. "And was it?"

Now it's his turn to be confused. "What?"

"Was it a smooth transition?" I bite back a smile.

"Yes."

We're awkward around each other...or maybe I'm just being awkward and he's just being himself.

I don't know, but I definitely don't want to stand here in the hallway with the happy people in the wedding photo staring at us. I'll take it down later, but for now, I head back to the kitchen, unsurprised that Noah follows me.

"You hungry?" I ask Noah before I think of the one thousand reasons I shouldn't.

He eyes the stove as I lift the lid and give everything a stir. "It's not poisoned," I add. "That I know of."

The corner of his mouth quirks. "Starving," he admits. "But Jamie's doing a bit of a workup on Scott at Dr. Prewett's request."

I hope he's just trying to be polite about waiting for the others. If he didn't want to be alone with me, he should have stayed down the hall with them instead of loitering around the photo shrine.

"It'll stay warm," I say because I'm hungry and selfish, then make quick work of readying two bowls for us.

As my hands move, my mind races.

The normal thing to do would be to sit down at the table or at the bar, but it seems both are too friendly and intimate.

I steal a look at Noah, and his eyes meet mine.

How is it possible for one man to have such a permanent intensity? Like he's telepathically forcing the world around him to move.

I don't have that skill, so I stab a fork in the middle of his food and make a show of sliding it across the kitchen island. Noah catches it easily before it can shatter all over the floor.

I hop up on the kitchen counter and shovel a bite into my mouth because I have no idea what to say to him, and it's all I can think about. I barely know the man standing four feet away from me.

I knew him once, at least, I thought I did.

The more I think about it, the more I understand he was showing off to the world what he thought it wanted back from him. Someone with a tough exterior, so untouchable and powerful that he had no choice but to be cruel.

We aren't friends, and we don't have a relationship other than being linked together by Maddy and Scott, so I recognize how inappropriate it would be to pepper him with questions confirming my suspicion.

It doesn't mean I don't want to, though.

I can't help but stare at his mouth, wondering what version of himself he's going to share with me next.

"Sorry," he says.

I don't understand why he's apologizing to me, but I'm still chewing, so I can't ask.

"I just got off a twenty-eight-hour shift," he explains.

It's then I notice his nearly empty bowl, the dark circles, and how generally exhausted he seems.

Is it possible that I just made Noah Washington, of all people, feel self-conscious? The idea seems so far-fetched, but I try to lighten the mood anyway.

"So you don't actually eat the food you serve patients?" I say because apparently I tease Noah Washington now.

He presses the back of his hand against his lips while he chews. I didn't offer a napkin or a drink, so I grab both for him. He nods in gratitude before he swallows, and I find the motion of his throat completely captivating.

It triggers something else in my brain, and I'm caught up in a highlight reel of Noah and his damn sculpted chin and the way his scrubs cling to his chest. And how that little dip on his shirt reveals just enough of his neck and collarbones. When the hell did I become interested in collarbones?

I shake my head and try to push away the temptation. I

hate how whenever you try not to think about something, it's the only thing you want to think about.

I've seen all the medical dramas, and I bet Noah has a line of women, like the psychologist who gave the presentation at Scott's award ceremony, who he takes in the on-call room. Maybe he does have a steady girlfriend he communicates with through his beeper, creating ten-minute windows for fast and delicious stand-up sex in one of the supply closets.

"I believe the hospital has an official complaint line for your grievances if you're unhappy with the color and flavor of Jell-O."

It takes me a beat to realize he's joking because he delivers the words with such earnestness, and I was stuck in my embarrassing and slightly objectifying thoughts.

"I'll look into it," I say.

He shifts on his feet. "One of my patients went into emergency surgery last night, and I promised him I'd be there for him the entire time. Usually there are a few slow hours where I can take a nap or step out to grab a bite as long as I have this with me. If they need me, they'll page me."

I glance at the small black device that's still clipped to his waist. "A beeper?" The amusement is clear. "I can't believe hospitals still use those. That technology was even outdated when we were kids."

"The batteries last forever, and I think it's easier for the hospital to send mass text messages at once," he explains.

"Well at least there's no need to relearn how to use T9 word for texting," I say lightly.

My first phone was a brick compared to the sleek iPhone on the counter.

In fact, I remember when Noah and his friends made fun of me for still having it during our senior year when they had all moved on to fancy flip phones.

I shake off the memory and resume my place on the counter.

I don't miss the way Noah's eyes flicker on my legs, causing me to glance down and stretch them out, confirming there's no errant crumbs or who knows what else from the hospital.

He clears his throat. "How long are you in town for?"

"Indefinitely."

The answer surprises him, which means he has avoided all celebrity news and gossip from nurses today.

"You're moving back here?" Noah clarifies.

He glances around the house and juts out his lip, as if to say that he wouldn't blame me if I wanted to come back. It's funny coming from him, considering the house he grew up in is probably triple the size of mine.

"For as long as Scott will have me," I admit.

Noah nods in understanding.

"I hadn't considered it until…" I trail off, biting my lip to stop the rest of the words from coming out.

It wasn't until Noah spelled out for me how the next few months were going to go that I knew I absolutely couldn't leave. It was the easiest decision I've ever made, even if it means watching Scott slowly deteriorate as his immune system weakens and his body starts to shut down.

I'm optimistic that I can keep him home and comfortable for as long as possible, and Noah agreed.

"I'm glad you hired Jamie," he says, pivoting slightly so I don't have to finish my sentence. "She's great, and she has worked for Dr. Prewett for almost twenty years."

I know this because I was the one who vetted her before I hired her, but I suppose it's nice he's validating my decision as a health professional.

She'll come by every day, even on the weekends, to check in and recommend additional visits to the hospital if need be, but at this point, it's best to keep him somewhat isolated, since his immune system is vulnerable.

"They should be wrapping up. But I'll be back soon to check on him." He pauses. "If that's okay with you?"

I take his bowl, waving him off from helping me clean it up, which in this case means dropping it in the dishwasher. "Of course," I say. "Anything for Scott."

Noah digs in his pocket and slides his card across the counter. "And if you need anything," he says. "Thanks again for dinner."

He's leaving, and I'm rooted in place, pressing his card into my palm.

Was the sound of his voice extra deep when he said that? Was he being genuine, or was he insinuating something more? How the hell am I a successful career woman with this much neuroticism and confusion swirling around in my head?

I leave those thoughts for my solo musings in the bathtub later, and I go check on Scott.

10

For the next few days, I settle into my new normal.

Scott sleeps for most of the day and night, but in between naps, I coerce him to eat. We also play cards, watch movies, and read. I manage to get him to sit outside by the pool for a little bit each day, and we talk about everything and anything while our feet splash around.

My mother is in and out, partly because things are still a little uncomfortable between the two of them, something I hoped would soon resolve itself, but also because she still works part-time at the nail salon.

I pay all the bills, but she likes the work, making people feel good, and the women she works with. I'm glad that she still enjoys it after all these years, but I still have no appreciation for when she mutters under her breath about the poor state of my cuticles.

On a hot, late afternoon, I venture out to the grocery store.

The back of my shirt, one of the random ones I found in

a drawer that says "HILL HIGH SCHOOL" and "GO FALCONS" on the front, sticks to my skin.

I wish I had access to my closet full of clothes I've never worn back in my LA condo. I only packed for a week, and I've been wondering if I should hire someone to pack up everything I left behind and send all my belongings to me.

Adam is still in the angry phase of whatever is happening in my career right now, so I let it be and focus all of the energy I want to expend on vanity into Scott's recovery.

Part of it is on a healthy diet, apparently.

This morning, Scott and I split a bag of sour cream and onion potato chips while we watched *The Price Is Right*. Nurse Jamie found us in a carb-loaded state on the couch, and...well, that's how I now find myself at the grocery store with a list of recommended items.

The last time I stepped foot into the local chain was when I still lived here full-time and Maddy was working her shift in the floral department, but I'm surprised to find that I still know where everything is in the store.

In fact, I have some sort of memory associated with the food on nearly every aisle.

The croissants in the bakery remind me of how Maddy and I stuffed our faces with them after a sleepover, courtesy of her employee discount. Same with the soft, white cookies with the pink icing and sprinkles—I throw them in the cart even though they weren't on Nurse Jamie's list.

I always wanted to eat those pre-packed lunches when I was a kid, but my mom scoffed at the idea of spending nearly five dollars on a few crackers, cheese, ham, and a fun-sized chocolate bar. Financial success means all sorts of things to different people, but to me, at this moment, it's the ability to buy one of each kind and try them out just because I can.

Grasping Nurse Jamie's list in my hand, I begrudgingly wheel over to the produce section and start working my way through her recommendations. I glare at the bell peppers as I bag them, realizing that I will now forever associate somewhat bland stir fry with Noah.

I breeze through the rest of the items, stopping for a few toiletries and giggling to myself as I sneak in some of Scott's favorite junk food items.

What's the point of dying if you can't live a little while you do it?

The smile on my face falters as my cart collides with another.

My heart sinks as I take in familiar black hair and green eyes. On Maddy, those features are gorgeous and alluring, even more so as she has matured into them, but on her father, standing right in front of me, they're sharp.

"Well, if it isn't Olivia O, coming back to her hometown crowd," he sneers.

A few people milling about look at me with interest, so I fix my face into a composed, disinterested mask.

Someone pulls out their phone to take a picture of me, and I ignore it as best I can.

"Ed," I say evenly.

I always referred to him as "Mr. Jones" as a child, but as an adult, I now fully comprehend the damage of his actions, the reason behind Maddy's bruised arms growing up.

He barely deserves to be acknowledged, let alone treated with respect.

I move to end the conversation by backing up my cart and turning it into the next available self-checkout lane. Of course, he doesn't let me go that easily.

"Heard from Maddy lately?" Ed says.

I ignore him and start scanning my items.

The machine keeps reminding me to scan my shopper card, but I don't have one, so every time I scan, I have to hit "Continue" on the screen to make it go away. It's slowing me down.

"Who?" I ask.

He scoffs. "Little thing, kind of looks like me, you know. Last I heard she got knocked up after I kicked her out."

I'm trying to locate the stupid numbers on the red delicious apples as quickly as I can, but my hands start to shake in anger. He definitely sees it because he stands up a fraction taller.

I square up and face him, taking in the fact that he's wearing a polo with a Gas Grub logo on it.

He works for Noah's family business. He's not in a simple T-shirt or those short-sleeved button downs that the warehouse workers wear, so I'm guessing he is high enough up in the Washington family's food chain that he does a lot of the dirty work.

Given his aggression and number of arrests, it's probably a mutually beneficial arrangement.

"I've been looking for her for a while but can't seem to find her," he continues, stepping closer.

I shrug him off, and thankfully, finish up the last of the items.

"Pass it along," he demands.

I catch one final whiff of his overpowering cologne and then he's gone.

I'm not even sure if he bought anything or what the hell he was doing here during the middle of a workday, but I'm so relieved he left me alone that I let out a full-body exhale.

"Everything okay over here?"

I turn and recognize the blond-haired man standing at the end of the check out area. We went to high school together, and we had a few common classes.

Thankfully, he's wearing a name tag. "Oh, hi, Dave," I say.

He bags up my groceries, and I follow the prompts and swipe my card so I can help him.

"I've got it," he insists, offering me a smile.

I return it, but I feel awkward standing here just watching him do his job. "How have you been?" I ask.

"Fine," he says. "My parents are good, and I'm getting a lot of hours these days with my management promotion, so I can't complain."

"And how's Leah?" I ask.

They were high school sweethearts. I lost track of their relationship after I heard they got engaged and were planning a big, outdoor spring wedding. The expression on his face falls.

I see that he's not wearing a wedding ring as he puts the last bag back into my cart.

"We...didn't work out."

My heart aches for him, but I don't say it. I'm sure he doesn't need my pity, and so I thank him and zip out of the store.

As I'm driving back home, I dial Maddy.

I've already broken my promise of seeing her more since I came back, but I know she'll understand as soon as I tell her what's going on, if Noah didn't already. Actually, I'm pretty sure that violates privacy laws, and I instantly dread that I'm going to have to rehash everything to her.

When I call her, she's excited to hear from me, and I invite her to dinner. Her car's in the shop, and Noah's at work, so I come by and scoop her up.

We get the car seat situated, and we're off, zooming back to my house with the radio on the nineties station. We laugh and sing along to "Champagne Supernova," and we're both surprised that it lulls Liam to sleep.

When I pull up, she lowers the volume. "I still can't believe you live here," she says. "That you bought this house. Remember how we used to dream of living here? Oh my gosh."

I laugh. "Of course I do."

"It looks just like I remember," she admits, craning her neck to take in the view.

"Is that a bad thing?"

"No," she says quickly. "But I don't know, don't you want to add landscaping or something? Maybe some flowers over here?"

I don't know anything about keeping plants alive. I've tried to grow herbs and succulents, all of which were promised to be easy to maintain, but I've killed every single one.

But it's an opening, and I'll take it. "Will you help me?" I ask.

Her eyebrow quirks up.

"Not with the actual work, I mean, I'll do it," I say, not sure why I just volunteered myself for manual labor and getting hot and dirty. "But if you could help me pick stuff out, I'd appreciate your advice."

"Of course," she gushes.

She continues spouting off information on perennials, light, and soil. I have no idea where she learned this information, but I just let her continue as I wrangle the groceries and she grabs Liam and the diaper bag.

My mother's home when we come inside, and she nearly shrieks when she sees Maddy and Liam, demanding to hold the baby. Because they live so close to each other, it's odd to me that they need to have a big reunion, but I guess their paths don't cross unless I'm involved, and I haven't been for a long time.

"Scott's awake," my mother informs me as she's cradling a fussy Liam in her arms.

"Scott's here?" Maddy asks.

"Scott's dying," he says, stepping into the kitchen.

Maddy can't tell if he's joking or not, but she takes in my tight expression and frowns.

"What? How? Why?" Maddy sputters.

"Leukemia," I explain. "Apparently he has known for months. I just found out last week."

Her jaw drops open, and she turns to give him a hug. He lets her fall into him. I know she can feel how thin he has gotten, despite his best attempts to hide it in baggy clothes.

When she sniffles, he chuckles. "Nothing worth crying about, Maddy. We all die eventually. I'm just beating you all to it."

I roll my eyes at how crass he is about this whole thing, but it works. She smiles and wipes at her face.

"Who's hungry?" I cut through the tension and start unloading the groceries.

The three of them and one adorable baby sit at the table, lightly chatting while I maneuver everything around in the fridge.

"What's all that?" Scott asks, eyeing the pile of vegetables on the counter.

"Nurse Jamie's recommended diet ingredients," I huff.

Scott wrinkles his nose until I toss him a bag of Doritos.

There's something exhausting about grocery shopping, and after all of this organizing, the last thing I want to do is cook. I want to join the rest of them at the table and enjoy a rare family-type setting, so I open a bottle of wine and order pizza, and everyone is happy.

11

"So you're really sticking around this time, huh?" Maddy asks.

I smile and turn my body toward her.

We're sprawled out on the poolside lounge chairs at the back of the house. Through the open window, I hear my mom gushing over Liam, who went to sleep for the night around my third slice of pepperoni pizza.

It's so peaceful here.

The night air is intoxicating.

Fresh, even.

The sky is almost completely dark, with the last remnants of dark blue casting down on us. Even then, I can still see a few of the stars and some of the little summer bugs floating around us.

"Did you know that in Los Angeles, they call them 'fireflies' not 'lightning bugs' like we do?" I ask.

She laughs. "I knew there was a reason I didn't like the west coast."

"Also, we're the only ones who say 'gum bands,'" I add sourly. "They're 'rubber bands,' apparently. And don't get me started on how often a restaurant doesn't have Heinz Ketchup..."

"Wow, now I'm never leaving."

I twist my hair up behind my head and lay back to face the stars once again. The slight breeze feels amazing on my skin, combatting the wine's warming effect.

We had such a light, fun thing going this evening, and I didn't want to tell her about my run-in earlier. Ed had a habit of ruining things, even if he wasn't physically present.

But it's better if she knows.

"I saw your dad today," I tell her. "He says he's looking for you."

"Of course he is," she sighs. "He's acting like I owe him money, but you know just as much as I do that I would never borrow anything from that man. Fucking asshole."

I nearly choke.

Maddy never swears, no matter how much anyone, especially her father, deserves it, and I think she surprised herself by saying that out loud.

We both break out into laughter, and I top off our wine glasses. I can't recall the last time I laughed like this, and it feels so damn good to be happy and relaxed.

"I can't believe I dealt with him for so long," she continues. "Honestly, these past few months have been the best of my life so far. It's like I traded a deadbeat dad for a blank slate with Liam."

Her phone buzzes, and she smiles when she flips it over to see who is calling.

"Who is it?"

"Noah." She snickers. "Remember when he gave you that nickname? What was it? Double-o-seven?"

"Because looking at me was a boner killer," I deadpan.

She looks at me with wide silly eyes and holds in laughter.

"Are you going to answer it?" I ask.

She squints at the phone and slides her finger across the surface. "Hello?"

Although I'm trying very hard to, I can't hear Noah's side of the conversation, but I can pick up his tone. He's all serious and business-like, and we're both tipsy and giggling like eighteen-year-olds. I love the contrast.

Maddy kicks her feet into the air while she talks to him. "We're at Livvy's...Yes, of course Liam is with me...Maybe a bit of Malbec...I normally don't, but this one is pretty good."

Noah says something else, and she looks at me. "Can I spend the night?" Maddy asks.

"Of course," I squeal.

"Should we make a big bed in the living room and stay up watching MTV and eating junk food?"

I don't get to respond because she remembers that Noah is still on the phone.

"I know...I know...Thanks, Noah. I mean it. Thank you. Okay. Au revoir!"

She ends the call and puts her phone on the table, now gripping her glass with two hands.

"Au revoir?" I can't help but ask.

"I don't know. It seemed like a good idea at the time."

"It reminds me of your beret phase," I say.

"Oh god, don't remind me."

"How could I not remind you?" I smile. "I'm just grateful that Goodwill offered so many styles and sizes."

She groans, and I remember the other interaction I had with my past at the store today. "Hey, Maddy."

"Hey, Livvy," she returns.

"What happened to Dave and Leah? They broke up, right? Last I heard, they were speeding along into marital bliss."

"Yes, but, like, a month before they were supposed to get married, she dumped him out of the blue. Through a text." She takes a big gulp. "A *text*," she emphasizes. "Could you imagine? I felt so bad for Dave, but Leah was always kind of the worst, wasn't she?"

"Kind of," I admit. "I always thought she was too bitchy for him, like she thought he should be grateful to be with her or something—"

"When he is such a catch," she finishes for me. "I know!"

I raise my eyebrows on purpose, wiggling for emphasis. "Oh you do, do you? Making out with him junior year really left an impression? Remember that?"

"Of course I do," she says. "I was the one doing the kissing!"

"Nothing says 'romance' like a post-shift make-out in the parking lot when you're sixteen."

She sips. "Those were the days."

"No they weren't," I say sadly. "They were actually kind of shitty."

"Really shitty," she corrects.

"Wine makes you vulgar, Madeline Margaret Jones."

We erupt into another obnoxious fit of laughter.

At this point, my mom comes out with snacks to help soak up the alcohol. We thank her endlessly and both stuff our faces. I wonder if croissants bring back memories for Maddy the way they do for me.

I bite into an Oatmeal Creme Pie, which I don't remember buying, but I now decide they are my favorite food. Definitely way better than stir fry.

"How is it living with Noah?" I ask her, tearing open another package with my teeth. "The truth."

Maddy chews and swallows a marshmallow. "It was really weird at first, but in a good way," she admits. "Sometimes I still can't believe how gracious he is."

I hum, and it's as neutral a response as I can offer at this point.

"He even lined up some interviews in administration at the hospital for me," she gushes.

"Oh wow," I say.

Maddy looks momentarily guilty, and I immediately assume she's about to tell me that she lied before and they've been having a secret love affair or something.

I press myself against the chair, as if that will help me brace for impact.

She runs a hand along her leg, not meeting my eyes. "So I saw his card on the counter..."

I blink. I expected a bomb, but it's actually an insinuation of something between Noah and *me*.

The most risqué our non-friendship has been was when I thought about him while naked in the bathtub. Even then, I focused on our interactions, not necessarily what he would look like if he joined me, how we'd be intertwined and how my legs would feel against him, and if his hands slid up...

"You've seen him a few times, right?" Maddy pulls me back to now, and her eyes practically sparkle with excitement.

"Not really, I mean, just for the ride home and at the hospital," I explain. "Then he came by to check in on Scott. That was when the card transfer happened."

When I finally managed to look at his card, I noticed his cell number was written on the back. He probably did that for all of his patients, I thought, but I still entered his number in my phone, wondering if I'd ever have an excuse to use it.

For Scott's sake, I certainly hope not.

"I think you should give Noah a shot," Maddy says like it's the most normal thing in the world.

"What?" I sputter, almost dropping my glass on the cement, but she's nonplussed.

"You're single," she reminds me with a once-over. "He's single."

"So are millions of other people."

Maddy rolls her eyes. "But you two have...history. Real enemies to lovers potential here, Livvy. You know I love a good redemption arc!"

"You read too many romance novels," I say defensively.

It's one of her very few vices. Maddy dragged me to the library on a weekly basis to check out the latest batch. Somehow, she even roped me into opening an account under my name so she could take more out at one time.

Of course, one Saturday when Ed came back to her trailer, slurring and angry, he tore up a book out of spite, and it was one of the ones under my account. I'm pretty sure I still have an outstanding balance at the local library.

"Oh come on and *Liv* a little," she complains. "You can't stay locked up here with Scott forever. Even he would want you to go for it."

I glare at her. "Has he told you this?"

"Well, no," she says. "But you both have changed since we were teenagers, and maybe it's time to act like adults and do...adult things!"

"I think you're romanticizing," I push back. "Noah was really awful to me for a long time with no repercussions, and now all of a sudden because time has passed and he has somehow reformed, I'm supposed to forget it all?"

"You're not supposed to forget it," she insists. "You're supposed to get to know him again, understand what he was going through, talk it out, and consider banging his brains out if he apologizes."

"He already did apologize."

"What? And I'm just hearing about this now?"

I shrug. "I understand that we were more naive back then, Maddy, but is that really an excuse?"

She looks at me, really looks at me. "You don't need me to convince you of this, do you? You've already justified this to yourself and are putting up walls in case he doesn't feel the same way."

"Why are you digging into this? It's not even a thing."

"But you want it to be?" Maddy fishes.

I sigh. "Let's talk about something else."

"Like what?"

"Like you."

"Me?" she balks. "Unemployed single mother. Boring."

"Oh stop it."

"Well it's true." She pauses and frowns. "I just thought by now I'd have everything more under my control, with more independence or accomplishments or something."

"You do have all of those things. You're an incredible mother, a kind person, and you just said it yourself that you have job interviews lined up."

She traces the rim of her glass. "Yeah, and all of it is possible because of Noah Washington."

I don't agree with her, but I get where she's coming from.

"Noah fucking Washington," I breathe.

"I just feel a little guilty," she starts. "Noah seriously has been so amazing, but I can't help but think that I should be paying him back somehow. I rely on him for everything, and I mean, come on, Liv. I'm almost thirty years old and barely have any money each month."

She chews on the inside of her mouth while she tries not to cry.

"I just feel so crappy sometimes, and here I am, raising another human to perpetuate the Jones' cycle of awfulness."

I'm floored by her words. "Maddy," I say as evenly as I can. "Just because it has taken you a little longer than some to get your footing doesn't make you nothing."

My vision blurs slightly, but I keep the tears at bay.

"You are the summation of everything that is good," I tell her. "You are nothing like Ed or anyone else I've never known, okay? Don't be afraid to take help from those who love and care about you because if any of our situations

124

were reversed, you'd be the first one opening up your arms to help out."

She smiles, but it's small.

I reach for her hand, which seems so delicate in mine, and give it a squeeze. This is a heavy conversation, and I don't want to see Maddy sad any longer.

"And now, let's get drunk and forget everything," I say.

"Cheers to that."

We clink glasses and slide right back into gossiping.

When we run out of wine, we decide it's time to make our giant bed in the main living area.

I have three guest bedrooms, and we strip all of the bedding from them. Our nest is so comfy that I have to fight sleep every single minute after I slip inside the layers of pillows and sheets.

At this point in the night, MTV is playing trash reality shows, and we narrate them with the sound on low, not wanting to wake the rest of the house. We switch to water because we are acutely aware that we are not as young as we used to be.

When I finally do fall asleep, it's the best and most wonderful feeling in the world.

But when I wake up in the morning, my head pounds.

It's a vicious wine hangover. My mouth somehow still tastes tart, but I swear there's a layer of sugar over my teeth.

I'm desperate for more water. I stumble over to the kitchen, realizing that I'm possibly still drunk. This makes me laugh like a lunatic, but the motion makes me nauseated. It's bright in the kitchen, and I shield my eyes, waiting for them to adjust.

When they do, I see Noah standing by the back door, holding Liam and a bottle, and I almost vomit from the surprise.

He eyes me, and I grip the counter so I don't fall over.

I'm still wearing one of my ratty high school shirts and cut-off jean shorts that are a size too small. I try to run my hand through my hair, but it gets stuck in the rat's nest.

Fan-fucking-tastic.

Of course, Noah looks as tempting as he usually does, but this is the first time I've seen him so casual. He's normally in scrubs or a suit, but this is my new favorite version of him, wearing a vintage baseball shirt with the old Pirates logo fading across his chest.

I'm curious if he buys all of his shirts a size too small or if the clothing gods just want to do me a favor.

His dark jeans, of course, are expensive and low on his waist, and I wonder how many women have had the pleasure of unzipping them and letting them fall to the ground.

My face flushes, and I'm glad Noah can't tell what I'm thinking. Or maybe he can, because his eyes are relentless as I go through the motions of making coffee and dry toast.

I nibble on a burned corner and immediately decide it's too soon to eat.

"Are you just going to show up in my kitchen expecting to be fed?" I ask him.

I'm trying to be cute, but my voice is a little low and scratchy, and in my head, it sounds creepy as hell.

"Your mother called me," he says, moving Liam into a burping position.

I look at the clock on the oven, and I can't believe it's past two in the afternoon. My mom had to work today, and leaving Scott to watch an infant probably wasn't the best idea.

"Oh shit," I say.

"It's fine," he reassures me. "It's my day off, and I was happy to come by."

He pats Liam on the back until he burps. He lifts him up so they can smile at each other, and it melts my heart.

I down the rest of my coffee even though it's still hot. "Well, I better go check on Scott."

"He's taking his afternoon nap," Noah says, keeping his focus on Liam. "We already had lunch, and he said he wanted to read some Whitman and doze a little bit."

The idea of the two of them having lunch together is odd, but I like the mental picture.

I'm wondering who made what and what they discussed when Maddy stumbles into the kitchen, looking equally disheveled but very panicked.

She takes in Noah, Liam, and me, assuring herself that everything is just fine before she whines, "Please tell me you bought croissants."

12

Nurse Jamie is pleased with my shopping choices.

I proudly tell her about some of the plant-based recipes I've been making. Scott pointedly winks at me when I glaze over the snack and treat sessions that are now a daily ritual for us.

She finishes up chatting with Scott and taking his vitals, and she asks if I'll walk her out. I find it strange, considering she already feels comfortable enough to open the front door and let herself in mid-knock, but I oblige her.

She tells me that physically, he is doing exceptionally well, but it's just as important to keep up his mental health. Reading and resting is great for him; he needs to remain optimistic and excited for life, not sitting back and watching things go by.

I thank her, but as her car heads down the driveway, I mutter a bunch of stuff about her being an amateur psychologist. She's right, though.

"So what do you want to watch today? Another soap opera? Reruns? A documentary?"

"I think we should go out," I say.

"Out? Of the house?"

I nod and try not to flinch.

He narrows his eyes. "Jamie put you up to this."

"Aren't you feeling a little stir crazy?" I ask, ignoring the reason for my sudden encouragement. "You have cancer, Scott. You're not in jail. Let's go out!"

"Fine," he says.

He tires easily, but we make it work and fall into a modified routine.

We eat breakfast together, wait for Jamie to show up, and then we're out, collecting lunch along the way and making it back in time so that he can still enjoy his afternoon nap.

Acting like tourists in our own city, we take a bus tour and then a boat tour.

We go to the movies.

He gets bored, tired, and cranky after thirty minutes at one of the art museums, so we drive through seven different fast food places and each pick out one thing to try and share.

We do a brewery tour and beer tasting, and I have to stop myself after the second IPA so that I can still drive.

We take a break one morning because I arrange for a local artist to turn the dining room into a painting lesson. Maddy and Liam come over for that one, and I take hundreds of pictures on my phone of Liam smearing paint all over the furniture and our clothing.

On a stormy Thursday, Scott and I sit at the table with the windows open, breathing in the warm and comforting scent of summer rain. He sips his tea while I work my way through a stack of mail, mostly bills and advertisements, but I stop at a postcard.

"Didn't you mention that you and Beth loved going to see shows at the Benedum Center when she was alive?" I ask.

He smiles. "She dragged me there, you mean, and I obliged."

"So you're telling me you wouldn't be interested in going to see *Bye Bye Birdie* on Saturday with me?" I pout.

"Do I have a choice?"

"Oh come on," I say. "It will be fun. We can get all dressed up and go out for dinner on Mt. Washington before and everything."

The doorbell rings before he can try and weasel his way out of it.

"Just think about it," I urge as I walk through the house to answer the door.

We're not expecting visitors, so I assume it's someone dropping off a package or a crazy stalker fan trying to break in—that's only happened to me twice in my career so far.

I crack the door and am relieved it's just Noah, keeping up on his promise to check in and visit Scott. "Come in," I say, shutting the door as he steps in.

"Is that Noah?" Scott calls.

"Hey, Scott," Noah says back.

They half-hug and start animatedly chatting about baseball.

Scott tried to get me interested in it when I was younger, but I couldn't find anything more boring than trying to get through a game, even if I had all the snacks in the world at my disposal.

I frown, realizing that he's probably far more interested in watching a pitcher perform than a classically trained singer.

"Scott, would you want to go to a home game with me instead of this?" I ask, tapping my fingers on the postcard.

It was a stupid idea, really. Scott hates wearing suits enough that he didn't even bother putting on a tie when he accepted his award at the beginning of the month. He'd much rather sit in tennis shoes, shorts, and an old shirt with a beer in his hand.

He readjusts his focus on me, and I hold myself still. The last thing I want to do is guilt him into anything.

"We can bet on who will win the pierogi race..." I try to tempt him.

"Let's do both," he decides.

"Are you sure?" I ask. "We don't have to."

"Noah can come along," Scott insists.

Noah glances down at the postcard, then to Scott.

I try to give him an easy out. "I highly doubt Noah wants to come see a musical with us, Scott," I start. "Plus, with his hospital schedule—"

"I'd love to," Noah says, eyes on mine.

I freeze, and my jaw drops slightly.

"Noah, can you help Olivia out?" Mrs. Parry, the guidance counselor, asks him.

"I'd love to," Noah says.

It's a Thursday afternoon.

We have a substitute in history, so Mrs. Parry rounded a small group of us to help out in the guidance office. Long overdue organization—aka free manual labor. But it's better than sitting in that stuffy classroom on the second floor, so I happily raise my hand.

Plus, I knew where Mrs. Parry kept a bag of candy hidden in the supply closet, so I volunteered to reorganize it. It was the perfect plan to waste the period until Noah Washington became a part of it.

He follows me down the end of the rows of offices to the supply closet. I'm carrying boxes and a garbage bag, and I set to work, reorganizing files and shelves, dumping old papers into the recycling bin. I'm conscious of Noah's every single breath, but I focus on the task at hand.

I'm waiting for it. "It" being "whatever Noah Washington is going to do to me," but it doesn't come quickly.

In fact, a good twenty minutes passes where I'm able to do enough work to justify sitting on my ass for the rest of the session, but Noah's already lounging on a stack of boxes, and I don't want to sit on the floor.

"Do you think this is what it's going to be like?" Noah says.

I can't even begin to fathom how this is going to lead to an insult.

I turn and look at him. "What?" I ask, ready to speed the process along.

"Do you think you're going to be stuck cleaning up after people for the rest of your life, while I, and people like me, get to sit here and watch it happen?"

It wasn't his worst, but it was rude as hell.

I'm just hoping to get a job when I graduate that helps me pay for community college classes or beauty school or something that's going to help me earn enough money to pay some bills and get my mom, Maddy, and myself out of the trailer park.

It won't be easy, that's for damn sure, but it's my reality. My dream, of course, would be to sing professionally—but that's as likely to happen as us winning the lottery or Ed staying sober for an entire week.

"Probably," I tell him because I know if I don't answer him, he's going to say worse things. Well, he's going to anyway, but I'm trying to hang onto some shred of self-preservation here.

I raise my chin up, showing that he hasn't hurt me.

It's an awkward move, more nostril-showing than strength, and he sneers at me.

"Maybe if your mom worked harder, you could afford better clothes. It's America, for shit's sake. It's not like you guys are stuck in the middle of nowhere with no options. You don't have to wear shirts with holes in them or embarrass yourself every single day you wake up."

"Said like a person born on third base who thinks he hit a triple," I mumble.

I'm somehow living in an alternate universe where I'm going to see a baseball game and a musical with the same person who once made a sport out of ridiculing me.

If I told my fifteen-year-old self that I would one day willingly spend hours with my bully and my English teacher, I would have laughed in my own face.

I suppose their camaraderie doesn't surprise me all that much. This version of Noah seems genuine and straight to the point, which I know Scott appreciates. I can't help comparing Noah to Jordan, one of the few males my age that I saw Scott interact with outside of school.

Jordan is very west coast in demeanor. He didn't have a

lot of patience for the slight differences and politeness of people in the midwest. Truthfully, he and Scott never really got a chance to know each other. They certainly didn't have a lot in common aside from me, and they never made an effort to spend time together unless it was at my insistence.

My then-husband focused on buttering up my mom, and she ate it up like her favorite meal. Jordan was, and still is, exceptionally charming. It works for him, landing him million-dollar sponsorships and millions of adoring fans.

I consider that Noah's primary audience is children, who are brutally honest and aren't afraid to ask tough questions. His life choices and career path speak volumes about who he is now as a person, not to mention that he is voluntarily spending his limited free time with a sick man.

I break out of my thoughts when Noah helps Scott stand up.

"Where are you going?" I ask.

"The faraway lands of the living room, kiddo," Scott says. "There's a two o'clock game on."

"But it's raining." Even I know enough about baseball to understand that they don't play in bad weather.

"They're playing in Atlanta," Noah explains to me before turning his attention back to Scott. "I have a friend who went down to the new ballpark just after it opened…"

They carry on without me.

I go upstairs to my bedroom and log onto my computer to buy us tickets. I use Scott's name but my payment information. I don't flatter myself to think that someone is going to offer me special treatment when my name comes across the computer, but it has happened before, and I really don't want that kind of attention.

With the door cracked, I can hear the sounds of Scott and Noah clapping over the rain outside my window. I smile, a big ear-to-ear grin, and head back downstairs to join them.

13

The pomp and circumstance of being in the public eye on occasion is one of the many reasons I am not cut out for it.

Most girls live for getting groomed at the salon, going shopping, and trying on new clothes. I find all of those experiences overwhelming and sweat-inducing, but I'm desperate for it now. Standing at the full-length mirror in my closet, I come to terms with the inch of brown roots and the realization that I have absolutely nothing to wear to the show tomorrow night.

I call Maddy and beg her for a spa day so I don't have to suffer alone, promising her that it's an early birthday gift from me and that my mom is more than happy to watch Liam. I don't mention that my mom also pointed out my "skunk streak" three days ago, and I've been ignoring her since.

After calls to three different salons in the area, I find one with last-minute openings, as long as we don't mind waiting between appointments in their "relaxation room." I roll my eyes, and I'm glad they can't see me through the phone.

I book us massages, facials, manicures, pedicures, haircuts, color sessions, and blow outs.

Maddy was reluctant to agree to this at first, but by the time we're pulling up to the salon, she's bouncing with excitement.

"After this, we're even for those bangs I gave you junior year," I joke.

She wanted swoopy side bangs that were in style at the time, but I ended up cutting them too short and asymmetrical. She had to gel them in place for two months.

"Deal," she agrees.

We're greeted at the door and ushered to the changing room, where we change into luxurious robes with matching slippers and lock up our belongings. Maddy and I both stuff our phones into the pockets so that we can document the day and be reachable if Liam or Scott needs us.

In the relaxation room, we sip on champagne before we're whisked off to our first round of treatments. We giggle a bit since the massage room is set up for a couple's massage. It's a very romantic vibe, but it smells divine.

After we get rubbed down with essential oils, we're off for facials in separate rooms. My esthetician makes small talk, and it's a pleasant experience, even when she's using the metal extraction tool of torture on my pores.

My entire body feels like pudding, so it takes me a few tries to get changed back into my street clothes. I wait for Maddy to finish up so that we can pick at the plates of fruit and cookies set out while we wait for the salon appointments to begin.

"Why don't we do this every single day?" Maddy says in a singsong voice.

She's practically floating across the room until she collapses on the couch next to me.

"I feel like I've Benjamin Button'd in the past two hours. I mean, look at my face. My wrinkles are gone."

I glare at her. "You do not have any wrinkles."

"Not anymore thanks to whatever that weird electric static thing that woman used on my face." She steals a few grapes from my plate and then helps herself to my cucumber-infused water. "Do you do this kind of stuff all the time with your friends in Los Angeles?"

I snort. "The few long-term friends that I have are still in the party phase. I can barely get them to agree to go to brunch with me, and they're always after me to go out clubbing with them. Neither is really my vibe."

"Well maybe now it should be," she says, leaning back and sighing in contentment.

"Are you going to do anything new to your hair?" I ask.

She purses her lips and flicks the ends of her hair. "I'm in desperate need of a bang trim, but I kind of like the overall shape of my hair."

"I do, too," I admit, but Maddy has those sharp yet delicate features that would shine even if she was completely bald.

"But why not?" she says. "You changed your hair, and maybe it's time for me to do the same. Getting rid of old Maddy and transforming into something new."

I smile. "Old Maddy isn't so bad, but I don't blame you if you want to branch out."

We're led through a few winding hallways to the room

dedicated to nail services. Maddy picks bright pink for her toes and yellow for her fingers. I don't think I've ever seen anyone with yellow fingernails before, but New Maddy is apparently an innovator, and I'm here for it.

"What color is your dress for tomorrow?" Maddy asks me as I'm still wavering on my choice.

"Oh, uh, I was going to run over and buy something tomorrow morning."

Her eyes light up. "No! We're going after this, and you're going to model at least twenty dresses for me."

I groan.

"You can't just pick any old thing for your first date with Noah," she exclaims.

The nail technicians watch us with interest. "Keep your voice down, Maddy," I insist. "And it's not a date. Scott's going to be there, remember? It's more for him than anything else."

"Right," she says, not buying it. "I'm sure Noah's looking forward to going to a *musical* and a *fancy dinner* with *Scott*."

The way she emphasizes those words makes me flush red, but I don't dispute it.

"I can't even remember the last time I saw you in a fancy dress in person."

"My first communion, probably," I mutter.

I settle on a neutral light pink, assuming that will go with whatever ensemble Maddy forces me into for tomorrow. I'm not the girliest girl when it comes to clothes. I keep it simple, despite my label begging me to do otherwise.

I'll occasionally use a stylist for big events, and it's

always a fight. I've never been comfortable in heels or in super tight dresses, but I'm aware that showing up to big events in comfortable ripped jeans would do more harm than good, even if they are more comfortable. I guess Scott has rubbed off on me in that regard.

Hell, I wore a pantsuit from the thrift store when I won my Grammy.

When our nails are in good shape, after a few sessions in the hand and foot dryers, we make our way back to the salon, where at least a dozen stylists work on various clients. I see the flash of recognition in a few people's faces, and at least two people try and fail to slyly take photos of me.

"If you want a picture, just ask for it," Maddy says, just loud enough to not qualify as "under her breath."

As we settle into our stylists' chairs, Maddy decides she wants an undercut and starts looking up different examples on her phone.

"So what are we working with today? Oh my gosh, Olivia. Hi!"

My gaze snaps up, and I immediately recognize Leah, better known as the woman who dumped Dave, Maddy's former parking lot kisser, a month before they were set to get married.

"Leah, hey," I say.

Maddy presses her lips together, and I can tell she's glad that I got stuck with her while a trendy woman with a pixie cut surveys the photos on her phone.

Leah pulls me in for a hug, and I oblige. "I heard you were back in town, but I had no idea you'd be here," she says.

"As you can see, I'm due," I joke, waving my hand up toward my roots.

She smiles, and she immediately switches into full stylist mode, running her fingers through my hair to get a feel for the texture. She asks me about my routine, and I don't miss her look of disappointment when I don't gush with excitement over big-name brands. I just use whatever shampoo and conditioner my colorist in LA forces upon me.

"Hmm, okay," Leah says. "Well you are feeling a little dry, so let's be sure to give you a nice mask after we color you, all right?"

"Sure," I agree. "You're the expert. I'm totally in your hands."

She loves that. "What do you think about going lighter? Like platinum blonde?"

I look at my reflection in the mirror. I originally went for this weird shade of gray blonde because I wanted something different, but I never really considered myself anything but a true mousy brown at heart.

"I just think it will look great with your skin tone, especially now that you have a tan," Leah presses. "The contrast will look stunning."

"I agree," Maddy jumps in.

Leah's gaze flicks over to her, but she doesn't show any signs of recognition, which disappoints me.

"Leah, you remember Maddy Jones from high school?" I ask.

"Of course," she lies, extending her hand.

Maddy shakes it politely, and then we're in full unglamorous mode.

For me, it's layers of foil underneath a fan while Maddy gets her hair shampooed. I thought Maddy would be sitting around waiting for me during the color process and then my own trim, but the woman doing her hair is so particular about creating an intricate pattern at the base of her skull that we finish up at almost the same time.

As Leah is putting finishing spray on my hair, a tall brunette comes and stands behind her.

"Hi, Natalie," Leah says, and I pick up on an undercurrent of nervousness in her tone.

I glance up and am struck by this woman's resemblance to Noah. She has changed plenty since my high school graduation, the first and last time I saw her, but the harshness and seriousness is definitely a family trait.

I glance at Maddy, and it's clear she wants to stay as far under the radar as possible when it comes to the Washington family.

"What brings you in today?" Leah asks her.

"I planned on coming in this weekend to have a quick look at the books, but when I heard Olivia O was gracing us with her presence, I couldn't resist stopping by today."

I swear internally. I didn't realize this was one of their many small businesses in the area.

Leah removes the cape around my shoulders, and I stand up to greet Noah's younger sister.

"It's a pleasure to meet you officially," I say.

Natalie nods, and the intensity on her face is so eerily familiar.

"I'm so thrilled you stopped by, and I hope you will make it a habit whenever you're in town."

She seems nice enough, but there's something about

her demeanor that I don't entirely trust. Maybe it's because of my past with Noah, but I'm just skeptical of the politeness.

Maddy slips out with a wave, beelining for the car to wait for me.

"Well, I'll be here for the foreseeable future, and Leah did a fantastic job, so I'll definitely return."

Leah's smile is as wide as can be, and I feel a little bad for judging her earlier by her high school personality. We've all changed a little bit since then. At least, I hope we have.

"Leah's one of our best," Natalie says brightly, and it's such a transformative statement that I'm taken aback by her change in demeanor. "Of course, all your services are complimentary today."

"No, that's not—"

"I insist," Natalie cuts me off with a genuine smile. "Someone uploaded a picture of you entering the salon earlier, and now we're fully booked for the next two months. Of course, we would happily move anything around for you if needed."

"Well, thank you very much," I say.

I stop at the counter to empty my wallet of cash for tips, then Natalie walks me out.

"If you don't mind me fangirling for a moment, I have to say that I love your music. Your second album in particular."

I smile. Some of my favorite songs I've ever written are on that record, but it was my least commercially successful work.

"You remember my brother Noah?" Natalie asks without a hint of irony.

"Of course," I say.

"Well, I used to drive him absolutely insane when he came home from college. Our rooms shared a wall, and he used to beat down the door to get me to turn it down." She laughs at the memory. "But one day I caught him watching a bunch of your performances on YouTube, and he was so embarrassed that I never brought it up again."

I force a laugh, and I glance over Natalie's shoulder to confirm that Maddy is silently screaming at this revelation.

"He even drove to Cleveland to hear you perform a few years ago under the guise that his girlfriend at the time wanted to go, but I know the truth."

I remember that show because it was the first one after Jordan and I got divorced. It was an emotionally draining night, but it was also therapeutic for me in some ways to put myself out there and focus on what was really important. Plus, it gave magazines something else to talk about other than our divorce.

Out of all the places I've toured, I never made it back to Pittsburgh for the exact reason that I didn't want anyone from my high school years to see me perform, so I privately groan at this information.

"Well, I better get back inside," Natalie says. "I meant what I said. Please come back anytime, and thanks for the free PR."

As I unlock the car, Maddy shakes her head and holds in laughter. I raise an eyebrow, telling her to keep her mouth shut, and we drive over to the mall.

14

One of the perks of spending hours getting layers of foundation, bronzer, and every other category of make-up available on your face over the years is that you pick up a few tricks.

Before arriving in Los Angeles, my idea of getting ready was smearing on eyeliner and mascara, and now, things are much more complicated. I take my time getting ready, singing along to one of the early albums by The Smiths and trying not to mess up my contour lines.

Once I finish running a flat iron through my ultra-platinum hair, I have just enough time to slip on my dress and get downstairs to meet the car as it arrives.

Scott is kind enough to offer a "Wow!" when I walk down the stairs and step into the chunky, and surprisingly comfortable, nude heels.

I run my hands over the silk material of my dress, which feels divine on my smooth and pampered skin. It's emerald with thin straps, like a slip, but it's floor-length and figure-hugging.

Maddy had to talk me into the dress. The material is an odd choice for summer, but we should just be going from one air-conditioned place to the next, and the high slit on the leg and dip in the back is a dangerous combination.

But now, seeing it all together, I'm glad I trusted her judgment.

"You don't look so bad yourself," I tell Scott.

Despite his protests, I got him into a suit. He refused a tie, but I kind of like the open collar look on him. He even shaved for the occasion, making him look younger and sleeker in one afternoon.

I choose not to dwell on the fact that his suit is a little bit big for him.

Aside from time, weight is another thing cancer has taken from Scott without his permission.

"Just make sure I look this good when you bury me in it," Scott says lightly. "In fact, I should probably thank you for giving me a chance to take it for a final test run before I'm wearing it in the ground."

I roll my eyes. "You're going to have to wear it for New Year's Eve when we go out for another night on the town like you promised."

"I'll do my best," Scott says, offering me his arm.

I want tonight to be special. With so much uncertainty, I'm trying to appreciate every single moment I have with Scott, and as much as it guts me to realize, I don't know how much time we have left.

This will certainly be the first and last musical I convince him to attend with me, and even though he's not terribly excited about it, it's a memory I know I'll think about for years to come.

Scott is contemplative but happy as we drive over to Noah's. He makes light chatter with the driver about our plans for the evening until I force him to have a selfie session with me in the back seat.

Most of the photos are him squinting at the screen while I make funny faces, which makes me laugh. I already planned on drinking at least two cocktails to survive this many hours in Noah's presence, but this is helping me relax, too.

Maddy tears out the front door when we pull up to Noah's house.

"Get out," she demands, waving her baby monitor at me like it's a weapon. "I need to see the full look."

"Wait," Scott says, then steps out and comes around my side of the car to offer me a hand. It's a sweet gesture, but I try not to put too much pressure on it as I slide out.

I've had training on how to pose on a red carpet, but it all goes out the window, and I shift uncomfortably as Maddy gasps, "Twirl."

I level my gaze with her.

"Twirl!" Maddy insists.

"You're demanding today," I say, laughing and spinning slowly.

Scott mumbles about how warm it is outside and lets himself back into the air-conditioned car. He takes the front seat, leaving the back completely vacant, and before I can argue, the front door opens again.

Noah steps out, and I almost faint at the sight of him.

If those hospital scrubs were crafted by the clothing

149

gods, then I can only assume this suit was handcrafted by Satan himself just to torture me.

The silvery gray suit is tailored to perfection, emphasizing his broad shoulders and chest. It's paired with a white button-down and thin black tie. His hair, normally slightly curly and messy on top, is slicked to the slide. I want to run my hands through it and make him as disheveled as I feel in his presence.

He looks classically old Hollywood handsome, and I'm now wondering if this is why Maddy insisted on this particular dress that I'm wearing.

She clears her throat, and my face flushes in embarrassment, only to realize it's for Noah's benefit and not mine.

He's standing still on the stoop, hand still on the front door, and gaping at me.

Noah sighs. "You look…"

I've never known him to be unable to articulate his thoughts, and that is honestly the best compliment I have ever received in my entire life.

"Off you go, you two," Maddy says, nudging me back into the car.

I slide in as gracefully as I can, knowing that Noah is following my every move.

"Hey, Scott, looking good," he says, patting him on the shoulder in greeting and falling into easy conversation.

I try to keep up with their words, but I'm so incredibly conscious of Noah's presence next to me that it distracts me. It's an injustice, really, for someone to look this good and not be stared at.

I try to keep my gawking to a minimum.

It's not like we're just friends going to an event together

because our agents think it will bring good promotion for the label. No, this is Noah Washington, my high school bully turned medical savior, and we have a complicated history.

This entire evening is the first real go at normalcy in a public setting.

I look out the window, focusing on the ever-changing scenery. Every time I come back home, I swear there's a new development or storefront. I mentally catalog a few other fast food places in case Scott and I decide on another round of drive-through samplings.

We cross two of the three rivers in the city, then we wind up Mt. Washington. I'm completely awestruck by the view at the top. I've seen plenty of pictures from this vantage point, but I think I'm the only one out of the three of us who never had a reason to see it until now.

"Daryl, would you mind taking our photo?" I ask the driver, gesturing to the outlook across the street from the restaurant.

It's a cloudy day and the city lights are just starting to ramp up, but there's a charming blue cast on the city at the point where the three rivers meet below.

Scott stands proudly between Noah and me, and I lean into him when Daryl starts snapping photos on my phone. He shifts around, taking pictures from a few different angles.

"I think I've got it," he says.

"Thank you." I check to make sure that they turned out, and I'm happy with them.

"There's a lot around the corner I'll be in. Just call me

whenever you're ready to be picked up and taken to the theatre."

We all thank him and shuffle inside.

I picked this restaurant based on the menu, but the ambiance is an added bonus. The interior is beautiful with floor-to-ceiling windows, showing off the view of the city below. I can tell by the design that it was built at some point in the mid-twentieth-century, but they've taken steps to modernize the interior with subway-tiled walls, modern steel tables, and sleek black flooring.

Noah steps up to the hostess stand, and it's clear the woman is not oblivious to his looks.

"Do you have a reservation?" she asks, batting her eyelashes.

He nods. "Under Ott."

"Oh, it's for Davis, actually." I step forward to correct him.

Her eyes go wide, and she somehow manages to completely forget about Noah. "Oh my gosh," she squeaks. "Olivia O."

Her voice is a stark contrast to the very formal button-down and black skirt she's wearing.

It's funny to me that out of all the times I've been recognized, the most common reaction is for people to say my name out loud. Like they need confirmation or want to remind me of my identity or something. Or maybe it's just a surprised reaction.

She starts on an excited rant about my music while flipping through a bunch of papers on the desk.

I give Noah a look that says, "This is why I hide my identity."

A smile tugs at the corner of his mouth. The hostess apologizes profusely that their best table isn't available, but would another one by the window suffice?

"Whatever you have available works," I say with a polite smile.

She rapid-fire asks me questions about what I'm working on now, when I'm going to finally do a show in Pittsburgh, and when the next album is coming out.

I deflect her prying as best I can while she gathers up the menus and leads us to a somewhat private location toward the back of the restaurant. Her hands shake as she hands over menus.

"You'll get used to it," Scott assures Noah once she's gone.

Noah doesn't look up from the wine lines. "I don't know about that."

I don't know if he means it's too odd to accept when a fan approaches me or that he doesn't plan to be around me enough to get used to anything, but I don't ask for clarification.

The waiter approaches, and thankfully, he's middle aged and doesn't recognize me or care enough to treat me any differently than he would Scott and Noah.

"Will you be starting with some wine this evening?" he asks. "I can make some recommendations for you if you'd like?"

I ask for his suggestions to buy some time so I can glance at the featured cocktails. I hate being the person who needs the server to come back multiple times just because I'm unprepared. Noah asks him a few questions about a merlot he mentioned, then he and Scott decide to split a bottle.

"Scott, you're not usually a wine guy," I say after I've claimed an Old Fashioned and the server has left us.

He shrugs. "I'm not usually this fancy, either, but why not? If you can't try new things when you're staring death in the face, when can you?"

"He's like this all the time," I tell Noah. "Talking about death like they're best friends."

"There's nothing wrong with being realistic," Noah says, agreeing with Scott.

I scoff. "There's also nothing wrong with being optimistic," I bite back. "Which Scott seems to be in short supply of these days."

Even though we're secluded, I notice a few people are taking pictures of me, including some of the staff, so I plaster a smile back on my face. I don't need a headline that describes me arguing with my dinner companions in a restaurant.

"Don't make such a fuss over me, you two," Scott tells us. "I personally would love to talk about anything else. Noah, maybe you can tell Liv your opinion on the Pirates' bullpen this season."

"Oh please no," I groan.

"Well then maybe you can give us a better answer than you give that hostess about the delivery of your next album?" Scott raises his eyebrows at me.

"So about those pitchers, huh?" I say brightly to Noah. "Baseball. America's favorite pastime. Let's go Buccos."

"And here we are," the server, my savior, interrupts.

He drops the lowball glass in front of me, then begins

the process of uncorking the wine, putting a small amount in a glass for Scott to taste. When he nods, the server pours for both of them and takes our orders. I pick a random pasta option on the menu and get a few side dishes for the table, and both men order steaks.

Maddy insinuated this was a date for Noah and me, but I suddenly feel like I'm the third wheel to Scott and Noah as they split the bottle, order the same entrée, and continue to engage in conversation without me.

"Are you still on a Whitman kick?" Noah asks him.

Scott nods. "Always. Did you get a chance to read the book I recommended?"

"I loved it, truly. Thank you."

"Did any of the poems stand out?" Scott asks him.

Noah considers it as he swirls the wine around in his glass. "'To a Stranger' resonated with me."

Scott chuckles. "That's Liv's favorite of his."

"Is it?"

"More or less," I admit. "Scott's always trying to get me to praise Whitman, but I tend to read more contemporary poetry, or at least collections that were written in the last hundred years."

"Who is your favorite?" Noah asks me.

"It'd be like asking you to pick a favorite patient, I'm sure," I say. "But probably Stephen Dunn or E. E. Cummings."

"And who's on your list, Scott? Aside from Whitman, of course."

Scott smiles. "Olivia Ott."

My heart always soars when he tells me that, but I

rarely get to hear him say it to other people. I grin into my glass.

"Poetry is how I got into music," I explain to Noah.

It's something I've told reporters so many times over the years. I never go into much detail for them, but the whisky is strong and dark, and it loosens my tongue.

"I never knew what I wanted to be growing up. Frankly, I didn't have the luxury of thinking about those types of things because my mom and I were always counting down the days until I could get a job to help pay the bills." I stop to look at Scott. "But Scott took an interest in me in his class. I wasn't that great of a student, but we did a poetry unit where we had to create poems out of newspaper and magazine articles, song lyrics, or whatever else was already printed, and I tapped into it."

"I remember," Noah says. "I was in that class."

I'm surprised I don't remember it. "Really?"

"Two rows behind you, one seat to the left," he adds softly.

"Oh," I breathe, and as I set down my empty glass, it's replaced with another one. "Thank you," I say to the server as he is topping off their wine glasses.

He ushers our food to the table, arranging all of the plates in front of us. Everything smells divine, like garlic and basil. The server grates cheese on top of my pasta, and my mouth waters.

Scott asks Noah about some of his work at the hospital, and we continue in light, easy conversation through the meal.

"And you're almost finished with your residency, right?"

Noah nods. "I start my fellowship next year, specifically

focusing on allergies and immunology. I thought being in the ER would be the most interesting and challenging, but after I did a rotation in pediatrics, well, I definitely preferred helping kids to dealing with people who blew up their hands from misusing fireworks."

"But why allergies and immunology specifically?" I ask.

"My favorite patient," he says, and there's a lightness in his eyes when he says it, like he's challenging my comment earlier that it'd be impossible to pick one. "He was six at the time and had been through four other doctors before he came to us with all of these terrible symptoms, which turned out to just be a simple food allergy, but it kind of caught my interest. I started researching it and then applied for the fellowship."

I'm fascinated by this revelation. I want to ask him one thousand additional questions about his work, to understand and appreciate his passion for helping others, a complete turn of how he was raised, but it's getting close to showtime.

The staff starts to clear the dishes, and I frown at Scott.

"Nurse Jamie would want me to remind you to eat your vegetables," I say to Scott, looking pointedly at the asparagus that's sitting untouched on his plate in front of him.

I slyly check my teeth in the reflection in the front camera on my phone, and I ask our server for the check.

"It's been taken care of," he says.

I look at Scott and Noah, who seem to be just as surprised as I am.

"Thank you for your patronage, and we hope to see you again soon."

Once he retreats, I groan. "Do either of you have any cash for a tip? This happened yesterday, too, at the salon, and I'm cleaned out."

"It's funny how when you're rich, you get a lot of shit for free," Scott laughs.

Noah smirks.

"I didn't ask for any special treatment," I explain while I text Daryl that we're ready for him. "People just hand it out, and whenever I refuse, it makes everyone upset. Just ask your sister."

"You went to Natalie's place yesterday?" Noah asks, dropping cash on the table.

"It was very enlightening," I say, not offering up any further details.

I still don't entirely believe that Noah is completely reformed—or that he used to listen to my music and drove almost two hours to see me perform, like Natalie said, but when I catch Noah repeatedly stealing glances at me, I'm starting to hope.

15

It's almost showtime when we arrive.

Of course, once my identity is revealed, they upgrade our seats from one of the middle rows to the third row of the orchestra pit. I catch a glimpse of the chandelier and lights on the ceiling before they dim, and I think about how many thousands of people have craned their necks to look up at them over the years.

When the show starts, I'm immediately lost in the colors, choreography, and singing. I've seen a few musicals here and there over the years, and I'm always awed by the performances and the people behind them.

I'm blown away by the love and dedication they have for what they do. I know from personal experience that doing six shows a week is no joke, and it's on another level when costume changes and dance numbers are involved. Thankfully, I usually stick to one outfit for each set I'm performing.

Scott falls asleep after the third song. Noah and I

exchange small smiles when there's a lull on stage and we both can hear his heavy breathing.

After Noah and I lock eyes, I find it difficult to pay attention to what's happening on stage.

I remain facing forward, but my mind refuses to focus on anything but the man sitting on my right. Out of my peripheral vision, he seems engaged with the storyline, and I'm a little disappointed he seems to be able to fall into the story while he encompasses all of my thoughts.

By intermission, I'm fidgeting. I need a little bit of distance, so I nudge Scott awake to let me into the aisle and excuse myself to go to the bathroom. The only bathrooms in the theatre are downstairs, so I walk as quickly as I can in my heels.

I'm accosted by two teenage girls, who ask if they can have a picture with me the millisecond I step out of the stall.

"Of course," I say. "But maybe I can wash my hands first?"

They laugh like it's the funniest thing they've ever heard. I'm just hoping they didn't hear me pee.

I hide out in the corner of the bathroom in front of the mirror until the five-minute warning bell sounds. The line for the snack table is only a few people deep, and I grab a bag of sour candies, wishing we'd had time to eat dessert at the restaurant.

Once I find my seat again and the lights dim for the second act, I watch Scott attempt to fight off sleep. He finally succumbs to it about halfway through the first scene, and I'm just relieved he doesn't snore.

"Maybe he'll stay awake for a baseball game," Noah whispers in my ear.

I'm startled by how close Noah is, but thankfully, I don't show it.

It's ironic that one of the characters on stage is singing a song with the lyrics "What did I ever see in him?" because I'm questioning my own sanity. I'm trying to be rational about my attraction to him, but it's hard when I am close enough to his lips to see the pronounced cupid's bow and how it's surrounded by a little bit of stubble.

He backs off, only slightly, and I look at him while I tear open the sour candy with my teeth. I dump a few in my mouth at once, enjoying the tartness.

I hold the bag up, offering it to him, and he doesn't drop my eyes as he reaches over, takes a piece, and slowly raises it to his lips. Whatever reaction he wanted, he apparently got because he fixes his gaze forward back to the stage, and I see him chew through the ghost of a grin.

Is he...being playful?

Or is he just teasing me about how clear my attraction to him is?

I'm not sure either scenario is ideal, so I focus on inhaling the rest of the bag as a distraction. My teeth rebel against chewing and my tongue burns, but the pain manages to keep me grounded.

I am not a woman who needs to ache in anticipation of the man sitting beside her. I don't need to silently will him to feel, touch, and explore every single part of me or tremble in desperation. The seventeen-year-old Olivia might have let Noah dictate her emotions, but this grown, successful, and independent version will not.

I toss the wrapper onto his lap when I'm finished, just because I can, and cross my arms across my chest, forcing his elbow off the arm rest.

Pettiness suits me.

Noah remains still for the next song, but when the next talking-only scene begins, he starts to shift toward me. It's a small movement, but I don't miss it because I'm so begrudgingly attuned to him at this moment.

I could probably use his inhales and exhales as a metronome.

Noah once again crosses the arm rest, the dividing line between us. As the audience laughs at what's happening on stage, he drags his knuckles across my thigh, tracing the skin exposed by the slit in my dress.

I gasp, but it's drowned out by those around us. I'm conscious of how many people are in this room while his hand moves, especially Scott, who is still dozing away on the other side of me.

The history between us should be enough to scare me away. It *should* be, but I don't know if it is. I grit my teeth, refusing to fall for this charade while desperate for an understanding of what he's doing.

Trailer trash.

Stupid girl.

Waste of space.

Double-o-seven.

But his hand is so warm against my skin. It has been too long since I've been touched like this, and I never would have guessed in one million years that it would be Noah making me want to open up and fall apart in the best way possible.

My heart pounds in my ears as his thumb slips underneath the fabric, and my body stiffens.

I have to look at him. I have to understand what he is doing and if this is just another game to him or if he is feeling this connection, too.

When our eyes meet, I'm not disappointed.

His expression carries an entirely new level of intensity as his gaze drops to my lips. His hand stops moving, but he's gripping my leg tightly, as if to claim ownership of some part of my body.

Noah *fucking* Washington.

We stay like that until the curtain drops and the applause breaks out.

When the lights come back up, I spring away from him and wake up Scott, who somehow managed to sleep through all of the cheers and clapping. I don't know if it's the journey, the alcohol, or the large meal that did him in.

Noah and I try to help him walk back to the car, but he shakes us off. He yawns every few steps, and his eyes are glazed.

"How was the show?" Daryl asks as we merge onto the highway.

"It was very...unexpected. But still good." I manage to respond with a straight face. "Scott, what did you think?"

He sighs and waves me off, and I sink back against the seat.

Noah and I sit closer than we did on the ride down, but there's a definitive line of separation between us. Tonight, in that theatre, was a turning point.

To me, it felt like a deliberate movement toward something new, deeper, and different between us, and I think it's the same for him, too.

If we were alone in the back of this car with a privacy barrier, I doubt I could keep my hands off him long enough to demand answers.

I want to touch him so badly, I'm actually in physical pain.

I sit on my hands to stop them from inching toward him, but I cross my legs at the knee, letting my ankle rest on his shin. It's so innocent yet so intimate, and it kicks up when he traces the skin around the buckle of my shoe.

I'm unable to form words, but he keeps up conversation with Daryl like there's nothing at all amiss. He's so collected, but I feel like I'm falling apart and he's only touching my goddamn ankle.

If our lips met, I would explode or melt or somehow manage to do both at once.

I'm the first one to unbuckle my seatbelt when we get back to Noah's to drop him off. "I'll be right back. I'm going to go tell Maddy goodnight and say hi to Liam," I explain.

"Take your time," Daryl says.

I tear up the stairs. The door barely closes before Noah slips in and shoves me up against it.

He pauses, just for a second with his hands on my waist. I must be giving him some indication to continue because suddenly he kisses me.

The weight of the years, the emotions, the desire between us hit me all at once, and I'm struggling to process it while coping with how fucking badly I want him.

It would be much easier to just use the internet, but the syllabus stipulates that our bibliography can't be from all online sources. I thank the librarian for helping me locate a book I need for my economics project and head back to the correct row of shelves.

The library's stereotypically quiet, so I hear the sound of my own gasp as I turn down the aisle.

Noah Washington and Kayla Van Baker are practically dry humping by the small shelf of economic and philosophy books. Her back is to me, so I can see him grip her ass with one hand while he snakes the other up her shirt to unhook her bra.

I step forward and reach for the book as quietly as I can, but Noah's eyes open.

He keeps my gaze but doesn't stop the motion with her. She moans when his hands move toward her front, doing some rhythmic movements on her chest that I can't see, and tilts her head upward so that he has better access to lick and suck her neck.

Noah definitely sees me shiver, and the involuntary jerk rolling through me snaps me from my trance. I grab the book firmly in my hand and make a fast getaway, so frazzled that I set off the alarm at the doors because I forgot to actually check out the book.

I apologize to the librarian, and she laughs it off, making small talk as she scans it out, but I can't mentally pull away from what I just witnessed.

Are they going to have sex in the school library? During fourth period? With other people so close by? More importantly, am I ever going to be kissed like that?

Noah pulls back, and his eyes are wild, wide like I've never seen them before.

"Olivia." My name is a plea. "Kiss me back."

I wrap my arms around his neck, bringing his mouth back down to mine. I part his lips with my tongue, needing to taste him, and he growls low in his throat.

We move together, and it's so damn good. He presses his hips forward, pinning me harder against the door and driving a friction that makes me moan his name into his mouth.

"Olivia," he mutters, shaking his head as if he also, simultaneously, cannot believe this is happening.

I try to sense hesitation or regret in him, but all I can see is the same need that's building within me.

Noah kisses my neck and glides his tongue along my exposed collarbones. I grant my own wish from earlier when I drag my fingernails through his perfectly styled hair, finding immense satisfaction in making him look as disheveled as I always feel around him.

He runs his hands over the silk of my dress, tracing in circles until he cups my breasts. Silk was a fantastic choice, but I want no fabric, no anything, between us. I need to touch more of him. I slide his jacket off his shoulders, and it sinks to the floor. I loosen his tie and tear away at the buttons on his shirt.

Noah smiles, finding humor in my urgency. I bite his bottom lip in retaliation.

His mouth is so hot on mine as I drag my fingernails over his chest. It's chiseled and divine, and I already know every single inch of the rest of him will be, too.

He wraps one of my legs around his waist so there's no chance of space in between us. All the blood in my body rushes toward my center, and I'm throbbing at the hardness I feel against me.

I remember I'm not wearing underwear at the exact same moment his hand slides between my legs.

"Fuck," he breathes.

I'm shaking in anticipation of this happening, but my body is moving on autopilot at this point. My brain doesn't care about the people in the driveway or our past; it's just me, Noah, and this feeling.

I arch toward him, encouraging him forward, and just as he's about to move closer, there's a clang in the kitchen. My gut reaction is to jump apart, but Noah's entirely in control of my movement at this point, and he's not letting me go anywhere.

Maddy is clearly mortified, not because she walked in on us, but because she was trying to sneak out before we knew she stumbled upon our little scene.

"I'm so, so, so, so sorry," she says, covering her eyes and sprinting back to her bedroom. "Carry on!"

I laugh and exhale, letting my head fall back against the door.

Noah releases my shaking leg back down to the floor, but he forces my chin upward, capturing me in another earth-shattering kiss. I press my hands against his chest to revel in the feeling of his heart pounding, knowing I caused it to beat rapidly.

I pull back. "Do you, um," I pause, and I can hear the undercurrent of nervous laughter in my tone, "want to do this again sometime?"

"Maybe without Scott or the musical or the audience," he suggests, brushing my hair back off my shoulders.

I bite my swollen lip and nod, smoothing my dress and hair as best as possible. Noah steps back and adjusts himself with a grimace on his face. I force myself to avert my gaze because one downward glance would be my complete undoing.

"Good night, Noah," I say.

He watches me leave with that familiar dark intensity.

I'm hoping the quick walk outside will erase all other signs of what just happened between us, but when I get back in the car, Scott takes in my ruffled appearance and doesn't hold in his laugh.

"Well that's that, I suppose," he hums.

I barely manage to keep my grin to myself the entire ride home.

16

Scott and I part ways in the entryway, and I already know I'm not going to be able to sleep for a while.

I should feel tired, but I feel alive, inspired even, for the first time in...I can't remember the last time I felt like this.

I slip off my shoes, leaving them in the middle of the hallway, and my feet move of their own volition toward the basement door. I take a few deep breaths, then I head down to the studio that I haven't seen in years.

When I created this space, I made it cozy and comfortable, trying to blend the panels that helped regulate sound in with the rest of the decor. I eye the computer and the other equipment, but I dig through one of the desk drawers until I find a notebook with plenty of blank pages.

My writing style has shifted over the years, but it always starts with putting pen to paper. Unfortunately, the only writing utensil I can find down here is a Sharpie. It bleeds through pages as I write, but I keep going.

My hand moves rapidly across the page. I'm going to be

angry with myself later at how loopy and smudged my words are, but I can't stop.

It's as if the words, thoughts, and feelings are pouring out of my body through my hands and this marker onto paper, so I go with it. I catalog everything I'm feeling and the beat of the words is steady.

I always write first, add music later, but now, I find myself humming potential riffs. It's a marvelous feeling.

My hand cramps, and I don't know how much time has passed, but I've already filled up this notebook, so I grab another and continue.

Eventually, my eyes begin to droop, and I stave off sleep for as long as I can, but eventually, I take a break, promising myself that I just need a quick rest before I get back to it. The words and ideas to at least a dozen songs are still surfacing in my mind as I slip into sleep.

My dreams are blurry.

The floor is hard on my back.

I need water.

My arms are cold.

I open my eyes, and it takes me a minute to run through the past twelve hours and how I got here. I sit up and groan while I stretch and again when I realize that I never put the cap on the marker, and it's all over the front of my dress, my arms, and the beige carpet.

Thumbing through the pages, I don't even care about the things that have been ruined or how unsatisfying my sleep was because of the words on the pages. They're jumbled and nearly incoherent, but they're there. I find a few lines in particular that I love, and I want to pick right back up where I left off.

I just need coffee. And a shower. And a change of clothes. And a massive breakfast.

The voices in the kitchen are too loud, but I face them head on, yawning as I step in.

"Double O!" Adam nearly screeches.

Am I dreaming? I take in his shiny light brown hair, now past his shoulders, and the three-piece suit he's wearing at eight o'clock in the morning. No, I must be having a nightmare.

"Were you in the studio?" My mom asks the question like she can't believe it's in the realm of possibility.

Adam practically cackles with delight as he pulls me into a hug. "You were working? Writing or tweaking music? How far along are you? How many songs? Did you get into a fight with a marker? Is that part of your new creative process?"

I lightly bat him and his questions away and pour myself a cup of coffee.

Considering the last conversation Adam and I had, which mostly consisted of him screaming at me, it's odd to see him completely elated and not using any curse words.

"What are you doing here, Adam?" I ask, sipping on the liquid caffeine.

Before he can answer, Scott enters the kitchen, and Adam's attention shifts over to him.

"Oh, Scott, I was so torn up to learn about your cancer diagnosis," Adam says dramatically, even though they've never met in person before. "Denise told me all about it and how devastated O is." He turns to me. "I told the label all about it, so I bought us some more time."

"More time?" Scott asks. He looks over at me and takes

in the fact that I'm still wearing the dress from last night. "Is Noah here?"

"Noah?" Adam's eyes shine. "Who's that? A Hill hottie?"

I collapse onto a barstool and glare at him. "Which one of your ten questions do you want me to answer first?" I snap.

"Ooh, someone's testy this morning. And here I thought you'd be excited to see me."

He's pouting, and I roll my eyes. I do feel a little bad about not calling him over the past few weeks, but he has been quiet, too.

"After all, house calls are not in my job description," he reminds me. "I'm very underpaid, you know." He shifts closer to my mother. "O refused to hire a publicist or a stylist at first. I've only been able to get her to work with a stylist on occasion, but usually, I'm all three."

"How awful for you," I mutter.

"Well, I still sometimes can't believe people actually like that weird computer music," my mother says.

Adam laughs. "Oh, I tried to get her to take piano lessons, but she failed miserably."

I look at Scott, begging him to help me out, but he shrugs and sits beside me with his own cup of coffee. Looks like I'm on my own for this—and rightfully so.

"Adam, what are you doing here?" I ask him again.

"Call it a wellness check," Adam answers. "Or a sanity check. Whatever you prefer."

I roll my eyes. "Neither."

There's a knock at the back door, and it's Maddy,

juggling a crying Liam and the diaper bag. My mother rushes to open it and takes Liam out of her arms.

Maddy thanks her and then gapes at my dress. "What did you do?" She looks at Adam and how strange his outward appearance is this early in the day. "And who are you?"

He extends his hand. "Adam Evans of LA Artist Management," he says.

She shakes it. "Does this mean Livvy hasn't been dropped from the label?"

Scott drops his mug on the floor, and it shatters. "What?" His voice booms.

Maddy looks completely embarrassed for the second time in twelve hours.

"I thought you had writer's block and were using this time to work through it," Scott accuses. "You can't give up your career for me, kiddo."

It's my own fault for not telling him the truth. "It's not like that," I try to explain, but the rest of the words die on my lips.

Scott's mouth is pressed in a hard line, but his eyes are soft, meaning he's not mad; he's disappointed, which is way worse.

Adam moves swiftly into crisis management mode. "Don't worry, Scott, this has nothing to do with you," he promises. "Actually, she's more than six months late on her deadline, so her ass has been in hot water long before your diagnosis."

"Thanks, Adam," I say flatly.

"Olivia," Scott chides. "Why didn't you say anything?"

"I just didn't want to disappoint you," I admit quietly.

"I would never..." Scott can't finish that sentence, so he squeezes my hand.

Scott had his reasons for not telling me about his diagnosis, just like I had reasons for not telling him about what I was going through in LA. Self-preservation is a strange beast, but we both cling to it, not wanting to put our problems on each other.

I'm annoyed he found out this way—and that he found out at all—but I don't regret keeping it from him. These past few weeks have been all about us letting go and enjoying our time together, and I think he would have felt guilty about it had he known earlier.

"So, give me all the details from last night," Maddy jumps in, breaking through the awkward heavy silence to give a pointed look up and down at my appearance.

Scott pretends not to hear her.

The doorbell rings, and I rub my temples.

"I'll get it!" Adam practically skips toward the front door.

I start to pick up the pieces of Scott's shattered mug. "I fell asleep in the studio," I say.

"Wait, you were *working* like this?" Maddy asks, jumping in to help me.

I shrug. "When inspiration strikes..."

Adam's squeal carries through the entire house, and I hear his excited chatter as he walks with Noah into the kitchen while carrying a huge flower arrangement in his hands.

"I assume these aren't for the dying man?" Scott asks.

Everyone laughs except Noah and me.

We're locked in on each other, and I'm trying to telepathically apologize for whatever this scene is. I don't know if he understands, but he helps Adam put the flowers in water.

I dump the ceramic chunks from the mug into the garbage and frantically try to fix my appearance in the stainless steel reflection of the microwave.

I'm a mess. My hair is all over the place, and my mascara is smudged. When I finish dragging my fingernails under my eyes to remove the black splotches, Maddy quietly slips me the hair tie from her wrist, and I sweep my hair up into a ponytail.

Nothing can be done about the Sharpie marks on my arms, though. They are semi-permanent tattoos, documenting my fit of creativity that was overpowered by sleep.

Noah sticks his hands in the pockets of his gym shorts and levels with me. "Can we talk?"

My heart falls to my stomach, but I keep it together outwardly. "Sure," I say.

I don't make eye contact with anyone as I step over the remainder of the spilled coffee and head outside. I close the door behind us, and we walk silently past the lounge chairs and grill.

Noah is in full brooding mode, which makes me nauseated.

I sit at the edge of the pool, dipping my feet in the water. The edge of my ruined dress sinks in, too, and I don't even care. The weightlessness and pulsation of the jets against my calves soothe me.

He, alternatively, stands over me with his arms crossed over his chest.

His body language tells me that he deeply regrets what

175

happened between us last night. He probably spent the night in restlessness, while I had my first creative breakthrough in months.

I don't say anything or make any move to open up the floodgates. Noah came over here with a purpose and with the most beautiful arrangement of flowers for Adam to monopolize, so I'm going to let him say what he has to say.

I have to just wait, but it's not easy.

He's wearing a simple gray shirt, and he looks like he's about to run away from this situation in his Nikes. He paces for at least a minute and a half before he drops down next to me, and when he does, I see his expression is pure pain.

"I hate myself for how I treated you," Noah says.

I finally open my mouth to speak, but he interrupts me.

"In high school," he clarifies. "Not last night."

The relief I feel in my entire body is so palpable, I have to stop myself from laughing because he is so damn serious in this moment, and I want to hear him out. It's not that I waited a decade for this, but that it seemed so out of the realm of possibilities that I didn't have a shred of hope it would ever happen.

"It's funny that you and Scott were talking about that project in English class because that's when I first noticed you," he starts. "At the time, my parents were reaming me for not living up to their unattainable expectations, like a freshman in high school was ready for the sort of responsibility required in their fucked up world."

He laughs bitterly. "The morning before the first period when Scott had you read your poem, the best in the class, my dad shoved me up against a wall and told me I was nothing. I carried that image of his eyes bulging out and the pressure of his forearm on my neck all the way to school. I sat in the back of that classroom in so much pain and watched Scott praise you, and I saw how happy you were, and something in me snapped."

That was the day it all started—my love of writing and Noah's hatred of me, two separate events and emotions somehow found a way to be tied together. I hadn't been able to pinpoint it until now.

"I was so jealous," he continues, grimacing. "I was the boy who had everything and was miserable, and you, by all accounts, had nothing, but were making someone in authority proud, and you seemed so accomplished. You were an easy target, so unassuming and defenseless."

Aside from my fluttering toes in the water, I don't move a muscle.

"I was angry for a really long time, and you took the brunt of it. I'm just so fucking sorry." He tugs at his hair, and it's even more disheveled than it was when I left last night. "The apology I gave to you weeks ago was not enough, and I just wanted to clear the air before this happens."

"This?" I ask.

I need him to be explicitly clear here because I don't want to live in ambiguity any longer.

"Yeah, whatever this," he gestures between us, "thing is."

Is a "relationship" too hard for him to say? Is a "thing" what people in their late twenties and early thirties have now? Just me and Noah and our *thing*.

I press my lips together until I no longer have the urge to smile.

"You think we're a thing?" I ask, dead seriously.

I'm mocking him because he's obviously carrying such heavy baggage, and all I want to do is float up into the air with him, leaving everything behind. I want to spend hours with him, relearning who he is as a person, and exploring the parts we never got a chance to.

Noah's gaze snaps over to mine, and I register the panic on his face before it morphs back into his normal, cool expression. "You're making fun of me," he says.

"I'm trying to, but you're so wound up, Noah."

He looks at his hands in his lap. "It took me a lot of therapy to work through all of that," he admits.

I wait for him to add to that sentence, but he doesn't.

He sucks air in between his teeth, and I feel pretty awful for trying to lighten things up.

I sigh, knowing that he wants me to spell out that I forgive him, but I can't. I don't think I ever will.

I've come to terms with what I thought really happened in high school, why he was so cruel to me, and while it feels good to have that confirmed by a professional shrink, there's nothing else I can do.

Noah made decisions when we were teenagers that set forth a path for me I might not have found otherwise. As much as I hate to admit it, without his torment and the wedge he drove between me and this town, I doubt I would have fallen as deeply in love with writing and its solitude. I certainly never would have left the trailer park when I did or have everything that I have now.

In a way, I am thankful for him.

It's hard to reconcile all of it, though, and I don't necessarily want to. I don't want to expend any more energy on the past. I want a future, one that's on my terms. No bullies or record labels or anyone else gets to decide for me.

It's time for a fresh start.

I eye the water at my feet. It's a little cold, but the sun heats the cement under me by the second. I don't even hesitate to slide in when the idea hits.

Noah watches me. "What are you doing?"

I hold onto the edge so that I can say this directly to him. "Have you ever noticed that we romanticize the idea of being by water? That all of our troubles will go away if we can just take a vacation by the beach and hear the ocean or sit on the edge of a dock with a cup of coffee, without a care in the world?"

I let go and start to tread water, which is no easy feat with my dress tangling around my legs, but we're having a moment and I suffer through it anyway. "Writers, especially, love to use water as a tool in their work because it's a sign of a cleansing, a new beginning."

My legs kick, and I move toward the shallow end. "I don't want to be a metaphor, Noah, but I want to start fresh with you, to figure out what we can be together and what this is between us."

I flutter my arms out, floating away from him.

Noah considers my words as he kicks off his shoes and socks, then empties his pockets.

I close my eyes and submerge myself in time to hear the muffled underwater splash of him diving in.

He doesn't surface until he's able to pull me into his

arms, and we both gasp for air and hold onto each other. I wrap my legs around his waist, pulling him closer so that I can run my fingers over the stubble on his cheek.

"Is that what you want, too?" I ask him.

"Yes," he says simply before his lips meet mine.

17

My hair is green—not a subtle only-in-the-light green but a fresh-cut-grass green.

I stare at my reflection in the mirror, somewhat horrified, and then promptly start researching how to fix this. As I read an article from a women's fashion magazine, I learn that had I rinsed my freshly dyed hair when Noah and I stepped out of the pool, I would have probably been fine.

But my mom brought us towels, and we sat outside to dry long enough for everyone else to move from the kitchen to the backyard. Before I knew it, it turned into one of those lazy days where everyone is comfortable and grazing on food and engaging in light, fun banter.

Adam admitted that he only stopped by because his flight to New York got rerouted due to summer storms. He was on his way to a concert in Manhattan for one of his "artists who stills makes music," and when the plane landed at the small airport near State College, he rented a car and decided to camp out at my house for a few days.

"It's the least you can do after all the shit you've put me through lately," he insisted.

I would have hosted him happily regardless, but he sure loves to twist the knife.

At some point in the day, Noah coerced me to attend a July Fourth party with him the next day. Not thrilled to interact with more people from high school and Hill, I tried to use Maddy's birthday as an excuse, but she jumped in quickly to assure me that we could just do a small, low-key dinner the night after.

When I finally made it up to shower, I didn't bother looking at my appearance until after I rinsed off. And now, I have *green* hair.

My fingers fly across the screen to figure out how to remedy my hair before I have to go to the party with Noah tomorrow. It seems like my best bet is to sit, once again, at the salon for hours on end.

I frown. Not only is that a version of hell, but I feel like I have already spent so much time away from Scott, and who knows how long the party will last tomorrow…

I glance up at my reflection in the mirror once again and try to decide if it's really that bad. Everything looks odd when you're standing in a towel, so I throw on a pair of shorts and an oversized sweatshirt and start posing. I flip the wet tendrils up on the top of my head, and I laugh at how awkward and self-indulgent I'm being.

When Scott calls me down for dinner, I give up.

"Fuck it," I say to my appearance.

Who cares what color my hair is or anything else about my appearance when I have someone I love who wants to spend time with me and only has limited time left on this earth?

I try to keep that mantra going through the next morning as Scott and I have our usual breakfast on the couch and game show television session.

After lunch, he shoos me away to go get ready so that Noah doesn't have to stare at "Kermit the Frog" all day, and I'm surprised to learn that he and my mother are planning to have their own cookout.

Adam still hasn't returned from his date last night. I text him to make sure he didn't get murdered and sliced up, and he responds with the middle finger emoji.

I also shoot a text to Maddy to wish her a happy birthday and tell her I can't wait to celebrate with her tomorrow night. She responds that she's excited, too, but more eager to get filled in on all of the Noah details I've been bottling up.

I brush my teeth and do my make-up, sticking with the basics since it's eighty-seven degrees outside, and put my hair in a twist.

Digging through my closet, I find another pair of dark, ripped jean shorts from high school and my old Converse sneakers. They will have to do, along with a super thin off-the-shoulder sweater I borrowed from my mom.

Feeling somewhat presentable, I pace around downstairs until Noah's car pulls up.

His eyes follow my legs until I'm climbing into the passenger seat, buckling in.

"Hi," I breathe.

He meets my gaze, and when he sees my hair, he can't help but grin. "Oh, Natalie's going to love that," he says.

I chew on my bottom lip. "Natalie is going to be there?" I ask. "I thought this was just a small group of friends."

He starts the car, grazing his hand over mine when he switches gears. Last time I was in this seat, I was both uncertain and angry, so I find it strange how naturally he reaches over to rub the skin of my thigh as we accelerate into the street.

"It is," he reassures me. "Natalie and Tyler throw this every year. Just a few friends and some of his coworkers."

"Tyler..." I fish for a last name.

"Tyler Edwards."

My stomach drops. I almost spit out the rudest things I can say about his best friend from high school who tormented me at the insistence of Noah, but we're starting fresh, so I go back to chewing on my bottom lip.

I'm glad I didn't open my mouth when he adds, "I was the best man at their wedding."

"Oh," I say. "But your parents won't be there today?"

The hardness rolls over his features. "I've barely spoken to them since my college graduation. Natalie has tried to be a bridge between us, but there's too much bad blood there."

I consider that. "All because you wanted to go to medical school?"

"All because I 'turned my back on the family legacy,' according to them. Natalie has been more than a suitable replacement for me. She has a knack for business, and I couldn't give a shit about it."

"What about..." I swallow. "All the illegal stuff?"

He squeezes my leg. "Another story for another time," he promises.

I don't push it, especially when he pivots the conversation to Scott and our morning together as we drive a few towns over.

For being the heiress to the Washington family money, Natalie's house is also pretty underwhelming. It's in a development, tucked away on a winding road and lined with tall hundred-year-old trees.

I'm confused by the sheer number of cars that are parked along the street, but I'm assuming there are multiple Fourth of July parties happening today.

Noah slinks his arm around my shoulders as we walk up toward the house, giving me the confidence to slide my hand onto his muscular back.

As we step up to the door, I notice the bottle of wine in his other hand.

"I'm such an asshole," I say. "I didn't even think to bring anything."

"You're bringing me, and I'm bringing the wine."

I roll my eyes.

He doesn't knock, but he has to drop his hold on me to open the door.

We're both taken aback by the number of people milling around the house. "Small group?" I repeat.

Part of me wants to turn around and run back into the safety of the car.

He reaches for my hand, and we wind through the crowd. A few people call for Noah's attention, and he waves to them with the bottle of wine.

I keep my head down, attempting to remain anonymous for as long as I can. The green hair might actually help me in this instance.

When we step out into the backyard, I begin to understand the allure for someone like Natalie Washington to live here. The views are stunning, and while the space is narrow, it goes back for acres. In the distance, I see a lake reflecting the sun.

If we weren't surrounded by one hundred people, I would love to do nothing but stare at the view.

"Noah," a familiar feminine voice calls.

I watch Noah and his sister greet with a half-hug, and he hands over the wine.

Natalie's eyes bulge when she takes in my hair, but she composes herself. "Olivia, I'm so glad you're here. You should have said something to me at the salon about you coming by today!"

"It was kind of a last-minute invitation," I admit, elbowing Noah gently. "But thank you for having me."

"Of course," she says, once again taking in my appearance.

I can tell all she can think about is the hours of bleach gone to waste.

Noah looks around at the scene of people, white table cloths, and catering stations lined up across the lawn. "Some party, huh? A little bigger than last year's, I'd say."

"Well, when Noah told me this morning that you were coming with him, I let it slip to a few friends who all of a sudden had cleared schedules," Natalie explains. "And it kind of exploded from there."

As if right on cue, I see someone attempting to take photos of me. I drop Noah's hand and fish my sunglasses out of my purse, sliding them on to act as a barrier.

"Which is exactly how I'm sure Olivia wanted to spend

her holiday," Noah says a little bitterly. "Being bombarded with people taking her photo."

Natalie doesn't falter under Noah's annoyance. "Well, good thing she has a date who is so charming and gracious and happy to help deflect," she snaps.

"It's fine," I say. "Natalie, where can I get that bottle opened for you?"

She turns back to me kindly. "I'll take care of this, but I recommend you try my famous red, white, and blue punch."

When she leaves us, Noah pulls me back to him. "We can leave if you're uncomfortable."

I shake my head. "Are you kidding me? I was once asked the age I lost my virginity on camera at a red carpet event in front of a dozen reporters and photographers."

"Don't flex too loud, your fans will hear you," he says lightly.

"Did Noah Washington just...tell a joke?" I balk.

"Don't get used to it."

We head inside to get some of the punch. I'm grateful to be standing in air-conditioning, even if it means sipping on a very strong mix of liquor and engaging in polite conversation with people from high school.

Some are tentative in their approach, while others come right up and ask direct questions about how "fabulous" my life is now. I'm well-practiced in answering these and just self-deprecating enough to indulge their curiosity while also kind of telling them to fuck off.

I'm grateful that Noah seems at ease beside me, watching me handle this on my own. Occasionally, he'll jump in the normal flow of conversation, and frankly, I'm relieved. I've had at least two experiences where guys I dated got annoyed at how much attention I garnered, but when I was with Jordan, I was always the one who stood silently while people gushed.

"If it isn't Double-o-seven," a booming male voice calls.

I stiffen immediately and turn to see Tyler Edwards.

The last time I laid eyes on him was our high school graduation. Appearance-wise, these past ten years weren't as good to him as they had been to Noah.

Girls loved him in high school for his height and size, giving him the nickname "Tyler the Teddy Bear," but now that we've aged out of those old versions of ourselves, his persona seems a little childish.

He extends his arms, waiting for me to fall into them for a hug, and I stare at him tentatively.

"I don't bite," he pauses, "unless asked to."

"I think a handshake will do," I say, extending my hand out.

He grasps it and yanks me forward, acting like this is one big joke as his arms wrap around me.

A few people laugh.

I shove him off me, and I'm glad I manage to not spill the drink all over my mom's sweater.

Noah doesn't move from his spot, but I see a redness around his eyes and a tick in the hard line of his jaw.

I down a sizable portion of my drink. "I see you're still the same after all these years," I bite out.

"Well, not all of us are lucky enough to win the fame lottery." He says it so casually, like it's not a punch to the gut. It's the same way he used to get away with all of his shit in high school.

What the hell does a smart, practical woman like Natalie see in this guy?

Fortunately, I don't have to spend another second thinking about the answer to that question because the woman herself pops back in, telling Tyler that one of their business associates is here and is looking for him.

He slaps Noah on the ass as he walks outside.

I chug the rest of my drink and help myself to another serving. "Best man," I say, tapping the edge of my cup with Noah's.

Noah shoves his hand in his pocket, and I can tell he's holding something back.

"What is it?" I ask.

I'm worried my jab took things too far. They were, and still maybe are, best friends.

He checks to make sure that no one is within earshot. "They're getting divorced."

"Who?" I ask dumbly.

"Natalie and Tyler."

I watch him swirl his drink around. "Why?"

He manages to laugh. "You have to ask that?"

I slowly sip my drink to compose myself, even though liquor makes me want to be more impulsive and reckless. "What's the hold-up?"

"Business and my parents, of course. They took Tyler in without question, and he knows a lot of the family secrets." He sighs. "One of the many sins I must atone for in their eyes."

I love how handsome Noah looks when he's serious, which is nearly all the time, but I'm starting to feel slightly buzzed, and I want him to come along for the ride, to lose that edge about him and fall over the cliff with me.

Cancer, parents, money, divorce, regret, it's all too heavy, and I have the perfect solution to combat that.

"Noah, can I ask you a question?" I actually hate when people say that instead of asking the actual question, but I am trying to pull him from his thoughts to focus on me.

"Of course."

I smile wickedly. "When is the last time you got good and drunk?"

He nearly chokes on his drink and leans back against the counter. "That's not the question I was expecting," he admits but considers it. "I can't even remember, it's been so long."

"And your shift isn't until tomorrow afternoon, right?"

"Yes," he confirms.

Natalie returns as I'm pouring liquor into shot glasses I found in the cabinet.

It's probably weird for her to see me taking charge in her kitchen, but I brush by it. "Want a shot?" I ask because I'm being polite, and honestly, it looks like she needs one.

Her mask is cool and perfectly done up, but it's cracking a little bit. Hosting a party is stressful enough, but trying to keep it together while your soon-to-be ex-husband is acting like a grade-A jerk is another thing entirely.

Before she even answers, I hand over a shot that's so full, some of it spills on her hand.

"You're getting Noah to be irresponsible?" Natalie asks with a smirk.

Noah sighs. "Just one will be—"

"I'm getting Noah wasted," I admit to her like he has no choice in the matter.

Natalie laughs, and it's a beautiful, warm sound. "Cheers to that," she says.

We throw the shots back. I cough because it's strong as hell. I glance at the label. Eighty proof.

We all chug the red, white, and blue punch as a chaser in a very uncivilized manner.

"That's it for me," Noah says, pushing the shot glass back across the counter. "I have to drive you home."

Natalie scoffs. "What's the point of having this many bedrooms if my big brother can't crash here when he needs to?"

"Yeah!" I exclaim, backing her up.

I pour another one, already knowing after this, I'll need a little break and maybe some food. Noah tries to deny it, and in retaliation, I attempt to grab his keys. He darts away, but Natalie grabs him by the belt loops and holds him while I fish in his pockets.

"Okay, okay, you win," he says, just as I'm pulling out the fob. "Damn, peer pressure."

The three of us stick together for the next hour or so, finding safety in numbers. We spend some time outdoors, but mostly, we stick to the cool air inside and the makeshift bar. I watch in awe as Natalie works the crowd, something I haven't ever really been comfortable doing, even with lots of practice.

"Why did I let so many people come over?" Natalie groans after a particularly long conversation with someone who is a fan of mine and an investor in her growing salon chains. "And why didn't Leah teach you proper post-bleach hair care?"

I laugh and bite the stars off an American flag cookie.

After the sun sets and the fireworks show ends, people begin to take their leave. Natalie seems relieved that the party is dying down, and there are only a few stragglers left when she starts yawning.

A very small and loud group of people surround Tyler in the yard, and I can hear their banter as Noah, Natalie, and I take a first pass at cleaning up the inside.

Once things are somewhat handled, we decide to have one more drink, taking it to the living room.

As we sprawl out comfortably on the oversized couch, Natalie abruptly turns to me. "Now it's my turn to ask you all sorts of questions."

"Bring it on," I say.

We're completely relaxed, and I wish it was light enough outside to enjoy the view. I'm satisfied and also more than buzzed.

"What's the worst part of it all?" Natalie asks.

Noah chuckles. "Going right for the jugular, Nat?"

"The invasion of privacy," I answer almost immediately. "I understand that being in the public eye means you give up some of your personal life, but when I started to get attention early in my career, I was wholly unprepared. Most of it was pretty tame, honestly, until I started dating Jordan. My mom used to get tons of hate mail sent to her, so I actually had to use a shell corporation to buy the house."

"Jordan Gravers," Natalie sighs. "I have to think an

NBA player is the best type of athlete to date. No outdoor games, free-flowing drinks, good music in the arena…"

Noah's face darkens, and he swallows a generous amount of punch. I watch the movement of his throat.

"It's not all it's cracked up to be," I say. "And anyway…I prefer doctors these days."

Noah quirks an eyebrow, and Natalie laughs.

"Unless you have a lot of twenty-year-olds sliding into your DMs that I'm not aware of…"

Noah pulls me close. "Not a chance," he whispers.

"On that note, I'm off to bed," Natalie says, rolling over to give Noah and me a group hug before she makes her way upstairs. "I'll make a carb-heavy breakfast tomorrow before I'm out the door. Pick any of the guest rooms. Tyler usually crashes on the couch in the basement these days."

I stay silent and completely rigid until the door closes, and it's only then, when we are truly alone, that I permit myself to look at Noah.

I don't know whether to gasp or groan at the pure hunger I see in his eyes, but it causes me to tremble all the way down to my toes.

He moves first.

18

Noah slides toward me. It's a slow, deliberate action that makes me feel like he is a fierce predator and I'm his defenseless prey. I'm more than happy with those roles.

One of his hands slides down my thigh, forcing me closer to him, while the other tilts my chin upward.

My teenage self, the insecure one buried inside me, screams for me to defend myself, to put up a wall between us, but I can't. This version of Noah, this man who has grown, evolved, and changed almost everything about himself in the past ten years, excites me.

He leans forward, and I close my eyes, expecting him to kiss me full-on, but his mouth hits my neck. I can't stop the sound that escapes my mouth as he pulls me onto his lap, giving himself a better angle for his tongue to move down in a slow line from my jaw to the top of my collarbone.

I'm an idiot for not wearing something to grant us both

easier access to this situation, like a dress or a bathrobe or a fucking paper bag.

When he starts to inch up the fabric at my waist, I pull back. He freezes for a moment, as if he did something wrong, but I smirk and lift the shirt over my head, tossing it aside.

My bra is plain, cream colored, and strapless—not one of my sexiest, but Noah is momentarily stunned by the view. His hands move before the rest of him does, dragging his palms up my sides, and when his thumbs slide across my nipples, my hips move of their own volition, grinding down into him.

I drop my forehead onto his, and we both watch the movements in fascination. We let it happen, entirely guided by the friction that is so fucking incredible I want to explode.

Part of me thinks I could do this for hours and just live off the feeling of what could happen between us, but I start to get impatient. I want more. I shift with the intention of yanking his shirt off, but when I take in the sight of his parted lips, I realize we've been moving together without even kissing.

His gaze drops to my mouth, as if he is thinking the same thing. I go for it, gripping the back of his neck to bring us together. He deepens our kiss immediately, and his hands move across my skin to slide into the back pockets of my jean shorts, pushing me more into him as he thrusts upwards. I moan, rolling my hips against him, encouraging him further.

I'm off balance, putting all of myself into the movement between us. He rolls me backward, and his weight presses me down into the couch. We barely break apart as his shirt slides off.

My brain tries to reconcile the hardness of his body with the softness of his lips.

I trace the lines of his chest and abs. I want more time together to memorize every single inch of him, but for now, I succumb to the urgency.

There's no shyness and certainly no need for the warm-up round with him.

I'm all in.

I slide my hands up his back, dragging my fingernails over his muscles. He pulls back to smirk at my dazed expression and pulls my bra down, giving him full access to my chest. He dips down and swipes his tongue around my nipples. I nearly pass out when he uses his teeth, a mix of pleasure and pain.

The rise and fall of my chest is quick, and I force a long sigh as I appreciate how good this feels. It's not lost on me that we're both mostly clothed, and I already feel like I could shatter at any second.

He keeps up the rhythm, and I already know that I'll probably have bruises tomorrow. Fuck, I want to mark him, too.

It's my turn to take control.

He is stunned when my hand slides past his waistband without any warning. I run my hand along his length, and I ache at how badly I want him, Noah fucking Washington, inside me. I touch him a few times until he's shaking like I was against his front door.

He digs his elbows into the fabric beside me so that he can hold himself up.

"Fuck," he breathes.

I feel so much power in the way he is reacting to my touch that if I wasn't already buzzed from the alcohol, I'd be totally drunk off hearing the low moan in his throat. He wrenches my hand out from his pants, a signal to stop so he doesn't become completely undone before it even starts, and I can't help but smile.

"You think that's funny?" Noah asks, his voice low and threatening.

I shake my head. "No, sir," I say as seriously as I can before a giggle escapes.

"It's your turn."

My eyes go wide when he unbuttons and unzips my shorts, sliding them down my thighs, just as the kitchen door opens and the conversation moves inside. There are a few walls that separate us, but it would take, maybe, ten steps for someone to see us.

My shirt is across the room. Noah realizes it just as I do, so he hands me his shirt to slip over my head, and I do so after I pull my bra back up. He grabs the blanket by our feet and fluffs it out, covering us completely underneath it.

I don't want to have a conversation with Tyler and whoever else is with him in general, but especially not while Noah's still impressively hard and my underwear is soaked.

Noah spoons me, pulling my back flush against his chest.

"Relax," he says in my ear.

I can't, but I have to because apparently we're just going to pretend to be asleep and hope that no one bothers us.

It's a really stupid idea, given how idiotic Tyler can be. I can imagine him running and jumping on us for the hell of it and exposing both of us to the remaining guests.

I just hope that everyone goes right to the basement or home through the garage instead of cutting through the house to the front door. I try to pick up on any shred of the conversation to give me an indication of where this is all going.

From the voices and laughter, I guess there are at least five people.

A bright, feminine voice suggests they play another round of drinking games, and I have to stop myself from rolling my eyes.

"Kelsey O'Hadley," Tyler slurs. "Are you trying to get me drunk?"

I remember that name somehow from more than just high school, as if she was the topic of a recent conversation. I nearly gasp when I recall Maddy's words from a few weeks ago: "He dated Kelsey O'Hadley for a while, but they broke up long before Liam and I came into the picture…she got fired from her bank job last year after it came out that she was stealing supplies from the company."

Perfect fit for Tyler.

The noise from the kitchen and whatever game they're playing fades as Noah traces circles on my stomach. I grind into him just because I can and it feels good.

I turn to ask if we should try to slip out and go upstairs to a bedroom, but he grips my hips to hold me still.

We're supposed to be asleep, I remind myself, but it just seems like a silly game at this point. Is it always going to be a game with him?

"It's your turn." Noah's breath is hot on the back of my neck, but I shiver.

I already know that what's about to happen is going to change things between us. I've already held his cock in my hand, felt how velvety soft and glorious it is in my fingertips, but there's something exceptionally intimate about the idea of him touching me there, penetrating me with his fingers in a way that makes me wish he would yank down my shorts and finish the job with him actually inside me.

Still, I'm unprepared for the first swipe of his middle finger on my clit.

I cover my mouth to stop from crying out. I can feel Noah's chest catch with a chuckle, and I immediately understand why he was annoyed that I smiled at nearly making him come in his boxer briefs.

He rubs me with one finger, and then two, and I writhe, wanting more. He obliges, adding to the rhythm. I arch back, pressing against him, and he increases the pressure of his hand.

My throat is dry, and I swallow because the anticipation is building quickly. It's not going to be long until I completely fall apart. It's expedited when Noah starts kissing my neck from the back, and I forget how to breathe. The movement between us is causing fuzzy spots in my vision. I fidget, silently begging him to move inside me, but he holds firm.

"Please," I whisper.

"Please what?" Noah asks. "Tell me what you want."

I'm furious and also incredibly, frustratingly turned on.

"I need…" I trail off.

"What do you need?"

He slips a finger inside me. I moan, and he pulls it out abruptly.

I want to cry. "This. You. I need it."

"So...fuck," he says, rubbing until I nearly break.

I whimper when he pulls one, two, three fingers in and out, and I'm so fucking close. I try to tell him this, but the words are incoherent as they leave my mouth.

"Fuck," he cries again, grinding into me again at the same pace of his hand movements.

His palm hits my clit at the same time his fingers curl inside me, and I finally find my release, screaming into my own hand as the world spins.

He jerks against me one final time, and my body goes completely slack.

We're both gasping for air, too loud for the normal cadence of two people who are supposed to be asleep on the couch.

The party still continues in the kitchen, which means I just had an orgasm by Noah fucking Washington's hand with his ex-girlfriend, his brother-in-law, and who knows who else within earshot, and I don't even care. I feel weightless.

Noah wraps his arms around me, and I sink in, trying to memorize this feeling.

"You are..." Words fail him, but I actually don't need him to finish that sentence to understand what he means.

"So are you," I say.

We resume the charade of pretending to be asleep, holding each other and enjoying every second of it, until we both slowly fade.

19

"Oh, you're still here," I say, not unkindly, to Adam as he stalks into the kitchen.

I smooth a layer of icing on Maddy's birthday cake, and he gives me the middle finger. We have a very professional relationship, obviously.

"I'm flying back to LA tomorrow morning," he tells me, grabbing a can of pop from the fridge.

He sits on a barstool, and a silence settles between us. It's not entirely uncomfortable, but it's still strange to see my manager in his casual clothes at my house in Pennsylvania, no matter how long we've known each other.

Adam has been with me since the beginning. I was his first artist at the management company, and we've kind of grown up together. I think that's why he has so much patience for me these days, even though I don't deserve it. I certainly don't bring in as much money as some of his other clients.

I finish icing the cake, licking the spatula before I drop

it into the sink, and I catch his uneasy expression over the containers of sprinkles I've lined up on the counter.

"Rainbow, chocolate, or pink?" I ask.

"Huh?" Adam says, shaking off whatever he was thinking. "Uh, rainbow. Nice for any occasion, right?"

I nod. "I also have to fit thirty candles on this thing."

"You should make a bigger cake," he suggests.

I laugh while he watches me shake way too many sprinkles on the surface.

His frown is evident from my peripheral vision, and it dawns on me that the entire reason he's still here is because he wants to deliver bad news in person.

"Spit it out, Adam," I say.

He drags his fingers through the condensation on the can. "The label's going to officially drop you next week."

I think he expects me to be devastated, and he rushes over to my side.

"I'm sorry," he says. "I tried to delay it, to give you more time, but when they found out you're running all over town here and not in rehab—"

"What?" I nearly shriek.

His face pales. "When I told them you were dealing with personal issues, they pressed me, and it was the quickest thing I could think of."

I level with him. "Instead of telling them that my surrogate father is dying, you told them I needed...rehab?"

"It wasn't my best moment, okay?" He sighs and rakes his hands through his hair. "I was just trying to stall everything for as long as I could because when the label drops you, my bosses are going to make me cut you loose, too."

That stops me.

I made peace with the idea of losing the label. In the back of my mind, I figured I'd return to my roots of publishing on YouTube and other streaming platforms like Maddy suggested or work out a deal with an indie label, but the thought of losing Adam, too, is like a gut punch, even if all he did for the past few months was yell at me on the phone.

"Fuck," I say.

It's an exasperated curse, and I much preferred that word when Noah's fingers were inside me twelve hours ago instead of in reference to the shattered pieces of my professional life.

"Sorry, O," Adam says.

He pulls me into a hug, and I let him.

Part of me wants to promise to fix all of this once Scott is...

I stop myself.

I can't even begin to think of that. I just need to focus on right now, finishing this cake and hanging up streamers before Maddy arrives. My throat is thick when we finally break the hug, and I clear it.

"A little heavy before a party, don't you think?" Adam says, attempting to make me smile.

"Adam, I really can't thank you enough for everything you've done—"

He waves me off. "Your big comeback, whenever it happens, will be more than enough for me."

We devote the next hour to transforming the dining room into party central with streamers and balloons, and I'm pretty impressed with our handiwork by the time my mother arrives home from work. Maddy and Liam follow her in, and I order pizza, with one covered in pineapple at Maddy's request.

I go to Scott's room to collect him before the food arrives.

He's sleeping upright in the wingback office chair. A well-worn copy of Whitman's complete poems dangles precariously between his fingertips and knee. I slip it out before it falls to the floor and jolts him awake.

Watching the rise and fall of his chest comforts me, and I enjoy the few moments of quiet solitude.

Scott has more wrinkles than I remember, and I have to think that it's the cancer and the weight loss, not truly signs of aging. I hate his body for betraying him like this, for somehow growing something toxic inside him that's slowly killing him. I'm even more angry that with all the money I have and potential treatments and new studies out there, he refuses to do anything but let it all happen to him.

"There are probably better things for you to do than stare off into space in the presence of a dying man," Scott says, jolting me out of my thoughts.

"Not really," I admit.

He chuckles.

The doorbell rings, and Liam starts crying at the sound.

"Party starting already?" Scott asks.

"Not without you," I say.

I hold out my hand for him. He stands, a little wobbly, and accepts it. He takes in the dining room and smiles when he sees Maddy.

"Happy birthday," Scott beams. "Thirty years old already."

She pulls him in for a quick hug. "Don't remind me."

We all sit and dig into the pizza straight from the box. I would have loved to treat Maddy to a four-course meal at some fancy restaurant, but that's not her style.

I'm already pushing it with the gifts I'm going to give her, so I didn't put up a fight.

"Noah's not here?" Scott asks me, helping himself to slice number three. "You chase him away already, kiddo?"

I roll my eyes. "He has to work today."

"He was super bummed he was going to miss the festivities and still a little hungover when he left," Maddy jumps in, smiling. "Seems like the two of you had fun last night..."

"Yeah, we did, but, uh, did you know that Tyler Edwards and Natalie Washington are married?"

"That's whose party you were at?" Maddy asks.

"Okay, I'm lost, fill me in," Adam says.

Maddy doesn't hesitate to catch him up on who all the key players are. He reacts the way he's supposed to as she regales him on more details of our high school years and how they fit in.

"Hell, Pennsylvania, does live up to its name after all," Adam smirks. "You all have been leading me to believe otherwise..."

My mom laughs like calling Hill "Hell" is the funniest thing she's ever heard.

"Too bad you have to head out tomorrow, Adam," I say.

"Oh no," my mom whines. "So soon?"

"The west coast *is* the best coast after all."

Scott scoffs, and we all lightly argue about how that cannot possibly be true. Adam huffs that I'm taking their side, not his, while Liam drools all over himself in the cutest way possible. I proceed to fill up the camera roll on my phone with all of his little faces, not joining back in on the conversation until we're ready for cake.

It's dark enough outside that I don't need to dim the lights, but the room is immediately brightened as I slowly walk in holding the cake that's nearly covered in candles. I set it in front of Maddy, and we sing a cheerful but somewhat pathetic rendition of the happy birthday song.

After we're all sugared up, it's time for gifts.

My mom gives her a bundle of free manicures and pedicures from her salon. Scott had me arrange a flower delivery to Noah's house earlier today, but he still presents her with a card that makes her sniffle with whatever he has written inside. I'm surprised when Adam steps out and re-enters the room with a designer diaper bag tied with a big bow. I give her a gift card to Natalie's salon and another to a local kid's toy store she mentioned once.

She holds everything in her hands in disbelief and says, "Thank you!" about one hundred times. It's far less than she deserves, but she's so grateful and touched that tears well up in her eyes.

"Better than your sixteenth?" I ask.

After she passed her permit test, we ate so many cupcakes in celebration that we spent the entire night on the couch with stomach aches.

"A little bit," she admits with a smile.

We all start to clean up, and I pull Maddy aside. "Can we head outside for a minute?" I ask her.

She looks at me quizzically but agrees. "Sure."

We drop on the lounge chairs, not totally unlike we did

a few weeks ago with very full wine glasses. First Maddy, then Noah. I'm a bad influence here, I guess.

Maddy sees I'm clutching two envelopes in my hands, and she tilts her head toward them. "What's this?"

"I have two more gifts for you."

"No, Livvy, it's too much already. The spa day was supposed to be my present! Besides, I would have been happy with just the pizza and the company."

Without argument, I hand her the first envelope.

She glares at me before she slides her finger across it. I started the process weeks ago, but I got a call from my financial planner last Sunday that everything was good to go. He emailed me a paper detailing the amount, the applicable numbers, and all the other relevant information.

"I can't let you do this," Maddy says.

"There's no 'letting me' do anything," I push back. "The account and paperwork are set, with Liam as the beneficiary."

Her hands are shaking. "You set up a college fund for him. I hear college is expensive, Livvy, but *one hundred thousand dollars?*"

"Well, I have it worked out that the money will go to the college of his choosing, and he'll get paid directly each year with a stipend for books, rent, and whatever else he needs. Tuition alone has tripled since we were eighteen. Who knows what state things will be in when he's that age."

Her mouth just hangs open in disbelief, so I try to soften it.

"I mean, I don't want to force him to go to school. If he doesn't want to, it will be paid out in three different installments at age eighteen, twenty-five, and thirty." Her face is unreadable, so I press on. "I just want him to have a better chance at things than we did, Maddy," I admit softly. "You can't be mad at me for wanting that for him."

"Mad at you?" She nearly shrieks. "All I'm thinking about right now is how I'm going to repay you for this."

I roll my eyes. "It's a gift."

She looks at the paper again and starts full-on sobbing, pulling me into her arms until she settles down a bit. "I love you," she says.

"I love you, too, birthday girl."

Maddy wipes her nose on the back of her hand, and she groans when she sees the other envelope still in my hands. "I don't think I can survive another gift," she laughs.

"This one's purely symbolic," I say, handing it over. "It's a key to the house. I know you already know the keypad and alarm codes, and I also know you feel like your presence is a burden to Noah and to anyone else, but please, Maddy, we're family, and I want you to stay here anytime you want. Move here if you need to. We can all take care of Liam when you get this awesome new job."

I stop talking when her lip starts trembling again. "Did Noah put you up to this?" Maddy asks.

"What?" I balk. "No? Why would he?"

She sighs. "I just didn't know if this was a ploy to get me out of his house."

"How many times have I told you that you're not a burden?" I say. "It's fucking wonderful to have you and Liam around, and my offer for you to move in here is nothing but pure selfishness on my part. You know I have plenty of room and resources, and I want to spend as much time with you as I can because who knows how long we have with each other. I mean, just look at Scott..." I drop off before I start to get emotional.

"So really, this gift is doing you a favor," she says.

I think she's mad until I see the lightness in her eyes.

"Yes," I press, encouraging her to continue with this line of thinking. "A big favor to me."

She laughs. "Is this weekend too soon?"

Now I'm the one pulling her into a hug. "Let's go back in for another round of cake," I suggest.

We push past all the emotion, and when we rejoin the group, everyone's fussing over Liam, who I swear is cute every single second of his life.

My mom pulls out a few of our photo albums. Adam is in hysterics at the pictures of Maddy and me from our teenage years. Scott provides commentary, but as I sit beside him, I can tell that his energy is rapidly depleting. He has good days and bad days, and I think that today is one of those in-between ones where he's mentally here but physically exhausted.

When his eyelids droop and his hands start to shake a little bit, I walk him back to his room.

He settles on top of his bed, not keeping up the pretense of staying awake enough to read in the chair, and he just looks so goddamn tired that it kills me.

I'm going to bring it up with Nurse Jamie tomorrow to see if there's anything that will ease him through it, maybe an herbal supplement I can talk him into trying.

"Did I tell you I bought Pirates tickets for us?" I ask. "Apparently, it's a division rivalry game, and they're giving away free shirts at the entrance."

He laughs. "I would have preferred bobblehead night, but that works."

"They really do that? Give away those creepy things at a ballpark?"

"They really do," he confirms. "Did you get good seats?"

Our definition of "good seats" is vastly different, so yes, I got him the ones he wanted in the scorching sun, but I also snagged box seats for when he'll need a break.

"Have you ever known me to half-ass something?" I pause. "Actually, don't answer that."

He smiles. "When is it?"

"The first weekend in August."

"I think I can live until then."

"Hey now, you promised until at least New Year's," I remind him.

He shakes his head. "Maybe Halloween if you're lucky."

I roll my eyes. "And miss out on Thanksgiving turkey and Christmas gifts?"

Scott sinks back into the pillow and closes his eyes.

"Hey, kiddo, will you read to me for a bit?" Scott asks in a quiet voice.

"Sure," I say.

It's the least I can do to make him comfortable. I pick up the book from earlier and crawl on the bed next to him, pulling up the sheets to tuck him in. I clear my throat and start speaking with the smooth rhythm of Walt Whitman's words, not stopping even after it's clear he has fallen asleep.

20

The next two weeks go by quickly, and unfortunately, I barely spend time with Noah.

He is absolutely slammed at work, pulling insane hours because of overlapping scheduling issues. He sleeps in the on-call room most nights. I even try to bring him lunch one day, but halfway through his turkey sandwich, he gets a page that causes him to run off, apologizing over his shoulder.

Maddy and Liam are on a very set schedule, and Nurse Jamie is thrilled to have people who are as regimented as she is. Scott and I bemoan waking up earlier, but we go along with it so that we can all have breakfast together.

"I think I want to start swimming," he says one day.

"Swimming?" I ask.

He shrugs. "What's the point of having a pool in the backyard if we don't use it?"

And that's how Maddy, Liam, Scott, and I started spending the slow and warm days of July getting sunburns and practicing our strokes. I order a slew of adorable bathing suits and floaties for Liam, and we all argue over who gets to steer him around the pool and make him laugh.

The day the label drops me, I don't even know about it until ten hours after the news hits. I'm so preoccupied with enjoying my life that I don't get to watch it fall apart on social media and gossip sites.

The day after that, Adam emails me the information about the dissolution of our contract, and I let it sit unread until I chug a glass of wine.

The following Tuesday, Jordan calls me to check in on my sanity and to share the news that he is going to propose to his girlfriend. We end up catching up for the better part of an hour. I'm legitimately happy for him, and I feel good after the conversation.

In fact, I decide I don't have a care in the world sitting by the pool.

I rotate between applying sunscreen, laying out until I'm too sweaty to function, and diving in. My studio stays neglected, but I do give my brain time to think creatively, and I practice my vocal exercises while humming the best summer tunes toward the sun.

"Is that the Beach Boys?" Scott asks.

"Yep."

"I'm half-dead, kiddo, can you turn up the volume, please?"

I laugh. "You're not half-dead," I say. "You're way past that if you're saying you're done at Halloween."

He splashes water up at me, and I squeal. "I'm thinking

Labor Day now. No sense in sticking around if I can't swim anymore."

"I'll heat the pool through winter," I promise.

Today is a good day, and Scott looks relaxed as he floats on his back. I rest my head against the chair and sing louder. Scott hums along a few times, but mostly he just listens and bobs his head back and forth to the beat.

I close my eyes and pretend like he didn't ask me an hour ago to take him to check out funeral homes on the next rainy day. He says he wants to be prepared, pick out his own casket or urn, and if I don't take him, he'll find someone who will.

We're doing our thing through the chorus of "Wouldn't It Be Nice" when the back door opens. I lazily open one eye, expecting my mother but see Noah.

I stop singing and sit up, very aware of how he is taking in my exposed skin, which is funny considering that his hands and mouth have been in places that this somewhat conservative bikini covers.

"Noah," Scott says brightly. "We've missed you around here."

"I've missed being here, that's for damn sure."

He's not dressed for the pool in any capacity, and he looks dead on his feet when he collapses into the chair beside me.

"How are you feeling, Scott?" Noah asks.

"Good, but I think I've gotten all the Vitamin D I need for today," he says, stepping out of the water and reaching for a towel.

"Scott, stay," I insist. "You don't have to leave. We can all hang out together."

He winks at me. "I'm ready for my afternoon nap with Liam now. I'll send Maddy down in a bit."

I frown at his retreating presence, but Noah grabs my hand, and I'm anything but sad.

"I love my job," he tells me. "But these past two weeks have been hell not seeing you."

"I'm glad you're here now," I say.

"And I have good news," he brightens. "I'm off on Friday night."

"All night?" I repeat. "Have any plans?"

"Well, I used to have roommates, but someone stole them from me…"

I laugh. "So you're complaining about having the combination of an empty house and a free evening. How will you get through it?"

"Well, when you put it that way…"

I don't see him again until he picks me up for our first official date. The restaurant he takes me to is new and nice. I smooth the front of the newly purchased red summer dress, grateful that Maddy talked me into going shopping after she saw the state of my closet when she moved in. My hair is still green, which makes me feel like a strawberry, but Noah tells me I look stunning.

We do our best to pretend as if we have no history so that we can get to know each other on a different level. I fill him in more on what my life is like recording and touring, and he closes the gaps for me on what happened with his family.

"So, after the ten-year-old showed up to the hospital, I had to get the police involved," he says. "Thankfully, the boy was fine, but he was able to identify enough to shut down my parents' heroin operation."

I nearly choke on my drink. "But your parents are...not in jail."

"Paying off a judge will do that," he adds bitterly. "I just couldn't be complicit in their actions any longer. It was bad enough when I decided to do something good with my life in college, but I finally had it then. Even Natalie is on the outs with them, but she's trying to turn all of their focus on legitimate businesses as much as she can."

"How are things with her and Tyler?" I ask, dipping the last piece of bread from the basket into my risotto.

"Complicated, as you can imagine. He's trying to draw the divorce out for as long as he can to maximize the payout, and my sister is considering just giving him what he wants so that he'll leave her alone."

"I wish there was another way," I say. "It sucks that he can walk away with what he wants. How long have they been together, anyway? She's, what, five years younger than us?"

He nods. "My first year of med school," he explains. "I came back over a break, and there was a party and...the rest kind of played out without my knowledge."

I take a sip of my wine, and I notice someone is taking photos from a few tables away. "Keep facing me unless you want your handsomeness on display for the world to see."

"What?" He turns and sighs.

"Don't engage, please, Noah," I beg.

He looks like he wants to tell the person to fuck off, but that will only make it worse. And when I tell him so, he backs down.

"I don't know why people think it's okay to do that. Does TMZ have a slideshow of people eating at restaurants?" He shakes his head.

"Actually, I'm pretty sure they do." I laugh. "But it comes with the territory."

"So back to family stuff," Noah pivots. "I've never heard you talk about your father."

"There's not much to say, I guess."

"Have you ever met him?"

"Only in pictures," I admit. "He took off when I was a baby, and we haven't heard from him since. I've always wondered if he would track me down when I became famous enough, but there's been no word."

"Might be a blessing," Noah suggests.

"Yeah. I think that's why my mother's relationship with Scott is so shaky. It was just us for so long that she was uncomfortable with the idea of a father figure stepping on her toes."

The server clears our plates and promises to be right back with the check.

"Has she dated anyone since?"

"No, she seems to generally distrust men in that capacity, other than somewhat harmless flirting."

"I'll keep that in mind," Noah teases.

I wrinkle my nose. "She adores you, obviously. Not as much as she loved Jordan, though…"

"Ouch," he says. "How can I compete with an NBA player?"

He's joking, but I'm serious. "You can't. You're above him in every way." I reach for his hand, and our fingers intertwine on top of the table.

I thank him when he pays for dinner, and before I know it, we're back in his car and heading toward his house. The anticipation buzzes through my veins, but it ceases when he opens his mouth.

"You up for one more outing this evening?" Noah asks.

"It depends what it is."

"There's this really cool bar that opened up by my place. We can walk there for a nightcap since it's still pretty early."

"Trying to get me drunk, Mr. Washington?"

"Just enjoying showing you off," he corrects.

21

We arrive on foot in less than ten minutes from his place, and the bar is, for lack of better terms, really fucking cool—something that I expect in LA but not the suburbs of Pittsburgh.

The lights are low, with exposed bulbs that give off a warm orange hue. It's all reclaimed wood inside, and they only offer local beer and specialty cocktails. I see a poster for a poetry reading next week, and I wonder if Scott will want to join me here.

We snag a table toward the entrance, and when Noah brings drinks for both of us, a woman gets on stage with her guitar.

"I didn't realize it was an open mic night," Noah admits. "Is it boring for you?"

I scoff. "Are you kidding me? I love this kind of stuff."

The woman on the guitar sings watered-down nineties songs for twenty minutes.

She's followed up by a saxophone player who admits

that he just picked up the instrument two months ago. He blows everyone away with his covers of recent songs, and I'm wondering why he's not more famous than I am.

The third act exclusively covers The Killers. His voice isn't the strongest I've heard, but I can tell he's obsessive about how he plays his instrument. I'm a little jealous because I lack their talent for instruments. My guitar skills are minimal, and my piano is outright embarrassing.

The crowd applauds each performer, and I down my second cocktail when there's a lull on stage.

I turn to Noah. "I want to do it," I tell him.

"Do…what?"

"I want to sing. Here. Tonight. On that stage."

He smiles, and it's wide and genuine. I plant a kiss on his lips before I leave him behind.

I approach the guy in the Killers shirt, and he recognizes me immediately.

"Holy shit," he gasps. "Olivia O! Can I take a picture with you?"

I laugh. "Would you want to do a song together first? Maybe I'll sing and you play?" I nod to his guitar.

"Hell yeah." His bright face darkens slightly when he adds, "I, uh, don't know any of your songs, though."

"I'm okay with a little more Brandon Flowers tonight if you are."

He's fidgeting at the idea. "What song? How about 'Everything Will Be Alright' or 'When You Were Young.' Maybe one of his solo songs? Something new?"

I laugh at his excitement. "What's your name?" I ask.

"Jack," he says like he is exceptionally proud of it.

"Jack, do you know the chords for 'Read My Mind,' by any chance?"

"Fuck yes," he says.

I grin at him and set my sights on the emcee, who recognizes me immediately.

There's apparently a defined list of who gets to sing on stage for the evening, but he pushes it aside when I ask him if I can take a turn.

I step up onto the stage via the side steps. Jack practically rolls on the stage from the front while I right myself at the stand-up mic.

"Hi," I say into it lamely. "I'm Olivia."

The crowd responds enthusiastically with claps and cheers. Noah's voice, in particular, is loud and cuts through the rest.

"My new friend Jack and I are going to do a song together." He beams beside me as he perches onto a wooden stool. "Are you all okay with that?"

Again, I'm a little taken aback by the excitement of the small crowd.

I laugh. "Believe it or not, I've never performed in Pittsburgh, my home city, before."

"We know," a random shriek meets my ears.

I chuckle. "Sorry about that, but I'm here now. And I'm going to sing a cover for you tonight." I pause. "It's a song I've loved for years, but it has taken on a new meaning for me lately. I hope yinz guys enjoy it." I smile at the Pittsburghese. The crowd eats it up.

Jack starts strumming, and when the small spotlight shines into my eyes, I lose all sense of my surroundings.

There's something magical that happens to me when I

perform. I seldom talk about it in interviews because it's so precious to me. It's like a sixth sense, another level of consciousness, but it's difficult to put into words, even for someone who makes a living through writing.

My eyes are closed as I open my mouth and start.

The pace is slow, delicious, and perfect. I feel the words in my body. Every note is like thick, smooth caramel on my throat.

As I hit the chorus, I swear the beat of my heart matches the rhythm of the song.

It's slow, deliberate. It's therapy, and it's working its way through my body. I don't want it to end, but before I know it, I've hit the bridge.

My chest is heavy with emotion as I open my eyes and sing the final lines of the song.

Jack fades out on the guitar, and the entire place is silent. I can hear the sound of my own breathing in my ears, so I step back from the mic.

Thunderous applause breaks out as the dim lights raise up just enough for me to see the crowd. There are phones everywhere, documenting the moment, and the biggest grin crosses my face.

I give Jack a hug, then he takes a quick selfie.

When I make my way back to the table, people stop me for photos. I oblige a few, but I have my sights set on Noah, who tosses a wad of cash on our table.

He's got *that look* about him.

We're silent as we walk back to his very empty house, but the tension is thick, and there's urgency in our steps.

His hand is heavy and firm in mine, and I can tell he's resisting the urge to break into a full-on sprint or pull me into the woods that line the street. I'm still flying high off that post-performance feeling, and Noah's intention is only fueling my adrenaline.

He unlocks the front door, and I fall inside. He rights me with his hand at my waist, pulling me toward him.

My natural inclination is to launch myself at him, but the weight of what we're about to do hits me square on the chest. We've agreed on a new beginning for us, but this means so much more. At least, that's how I feel. I'm not one to spread my legs on a whim, and it's not lost on me that it's Noah fucking Washington I want between them.

I wait for the bad memories to surface, but none do.

I take it as a good sign and tug at the front of his shirt, wanting to feel something tangible in between my fingers. I need to make sure that I'm not hallucinating these feelings between us.

"You are incredible, Olivia Ott." Noah runs his thumb over my bottom lip. "Watching you tonight…it's like you shared a piece of yourself."

I bite his thumb gently, and when I release it, I ask, "Better than I was in Cleveland?"

His eyebrows tick upward. "How do you know about that?"

"Natalie," I answer.

"Of course," he sighs.

It's taken me some time to recalibrate my brain to this version of Noah, but the honest truth is that there is something about him that has always enticed me, even in his cruelest moments.

I've had plenty of free time lately to overanalyze our interactions, and the more I piece it together, the more I wonder how long he's buried these feelings for me somewhere inside him.

"When did it change for you?" It's a whisper, but it's the most important question I've ever asked him. "When did your feelings for me change?"

I'm cocooned in his arms, and we're standing in the same spot where we first kissed those weeks ago, completely lust-driven.

I still feel that way about him, but I need more this time; I need to understand his mind, to know the truth about his feelings for me.

He stares directly into my eyes when he says, "When you left."

I didn't expect it, but I'm not entirely surprised by it.

"How?"

He shakes his head, as if he hates that I'm making him do this now and that it's too painful for him to pull up again.

"Help me understand, Noah," I urge.

"I always saw you, Olivia. Long before that poetry assignment, I knew you were too much for this small town, for all of us, but it took you leaving it all behind to really realize how special you were, and it tore me up. Like I had missed my chance to experience something and to be with someone completely extraordinary. It caused me to rethink my life trajectory completely."

My heart pounds, and he slides his hands up my neck, fingers locked in my hair. I can't look anywhere else even if I want to.

"I kept tabs on you throughout the years, following your career and those stupid gossip magazines, and I lost myself in work and everything else. But whenever your song came on the radio or someone at work bragged about interacting with you at some point, it did something to me that I didn't completely understand until you came back here and I saw you on stage presenting Scott's award. So beautiful and accomplished and poised and everything I shouldn't have missed out on all those years."

He leans down closer toward me, and the next words are light against my lips.

"And now…you're just so much more than I ever could have imagined."

Without hesitation, I kiss him.

It's slow, and I soften into him completely. His hands remain in my hair, as if holding onto me is the only way he is keeping himself together.

I walk backward up the stairs, and he follows, barely breaking his mouth from mine as we move toward his bedroom.

When the backs of my knees hit the edge of the mattress, he eases his grasp so that he can slowly unzip the back of my dress. I feel every inch of it move down my spine. It drops to my feet, and I undo the buttons of his shirt, slow and teasing. He shrugs it off while I lick his bare chest.

He unclasps my bra.

"So much more," he repeats.

I undo his belt and his pants hit the floor.

We stare into each other's eyes as we slide down our own underwear and face each other, bared completely in body and in mind.

He clears his throat. "Being a medical professional and all…I have to ask…"

"I'm on the pill," I say, already knowing where this is heading. "And I'm clean."

His eyes flash. "Me too."

Our lips meet once more, and it's happening.

Between us.

Right now.

We've had nothing but foreplay for weeks, or years, depending on how you look at it, and we're both ready for this moment.

He lowers me onto the bed.

We tangle up together, with his hands pinning mine above my head and my legs wrapped around his waist. Our eyes are locked as he rolls his hips forward, and I cry out. He bites his lip when he glances down, watching himself enter me inch by glorious inch.

The words that come out of my mouth don't necessarily make sense, but it's some combination of swear words and both of us saying, "More."

Noah sets the pace, and to some degree, I'm just along for the ride. Every single second feels better than the last, and I don't care to stop this movement for the rest of my life.

I want to run my fingernails down his back and grip my hands on his ass, but he still pins me down. "Noah," I say, my voice unrecognizable. "Let me explore."

He nods, and our mouths are together as I touch him everywhere I can reach.

The pace picks up, and fuck, the friction and the fullness, and…

"So good," Noah says between clenched teeth.

He nips at my neck, and I slide my hand further down, continuing to build toward this release. As his hips move, I circle my fingers on my swollen clit. Noah moans when he sees the movement, pumping in and out faster.

"I'm close," I tell him.

His tongue darts over one of my nipples, and I arch into his mouth.

It's agony and everything all at once. We both let go and lose ourselves in the feeling and the sounds and waves that crash down on us until we're both left breathless, holding onto each other like we always should have been.

22

When I wake up, the first thing I see is Noah scrolling on his phone, smirk evident.

Well, it's technically the second time I've woken up this morning—the first was to Noah's hands and mouth moving downwards along my body, and I definitely think that is my preferred way to start the day.

"You're viral," Noah says, holding up the phone for me to see.

I squint until I adjust to the light, and then I see that the somewhat shaky video has more than one million views already.

Adam's no longer my manager, but I'm not entirely surprised to see a few missed calls and text messages from him.

GIRLLLLLLLLLL
WHERE HAS THIS ENERGY BEEN THE PAST YEAR?!?!?!
NO. THE PAST DECADE????
OLD TOWN, NEW YOU

CALL ME!!!!!!!!!

I roll my eyes and set my phone aside, retreating back under the sheet to curl up against Noah.

He clears his throat. "So, out of everything we've talked about, I've never asked...what are your plans for all of this?"

"Is that your polite way of asking what the hell I'm going to do to reignite the career that I single-handedly burned to the ground?" I ask.

"Not in so many words," he says, pulling me closer.

I swallow. "I haven't thought about it. Well, that's a lie, actually. I have, but I've been putting it off because once I can give my full attention to it, it means that Scott..."

Noah kisses my forehead, and I lay my head on his chest.

"I don't know Scott extremely well, but I would assume that he wouldn't want you to put your career on hold just to wait around for him."

I laugh. "You're right."

"You can't take a break from reality, Olivia."

"A little summer break doesn't hurt anything."

"It doesn't, but you're just procrastinating and putting off your problems," he says gently. "They'll still be there in the fall."

He's right, and it's funny because as close as I feel to him at this moment, I'm not ready to have this conversation with him yet. I want to stay in the blissful state, ignoring the career that's waiting for me on the west coast.

I yawn. "Well, focusing on the immediate need at hand," I start. "I need a shower. And breakfast."

The glint in his eyes is clear. "I can help you with both of those things..."

He chases me into the shower, and we get dirty again before we get clean.

After a quick breakfast of avocado toast and coffee, Noah's off to the hospital, and I'm back at home in time for an afternoon of nothingness with Scott by the pool.

I hate to wash off the smell of Noah's soap, but I'm looking forward to a lazy day interspersed with a nap or two.

I change into my swimsuit and cover-up, but Maddy intercepts me before I can check on Scott.

She makes me rehash every single detail of my previous night with her no matter how much she blushes. She slathers sunscreen on Liam, who understands nothing but loves Maddy's reactions to what I'm telling her.

"So when are you going to see him again?" Maddy asks me.

I shrug. "We didn't compare calendars just yet."

She smiles, lost in her own thoughts, and after a beat, she starts laughing.

"What?"

"I guess Double-o-seven isn't a boner killer after all," she blurts out. "If anything, it's the opposite."

"I can't believe you would say such vulgar things in front of your *son*," I tease.

I grab the bottle of sunscreen and head toward Scott's room, happy as can be, but my mother storms out, eyes brimming with tears.

"What?" I demand, but she ignores me and heads upstairs.

My mind races to the worst of all circumstances, but even I know as weird as things have always been between them, if he was dying or hurt, my mother wouldn't flee and brush me off.

When I push the door open, waving the bottle in my hand, the excitement of our afternoon ahead vanishes. Scott is sitting in the chair, flipping through a book, but his eyes are unfocused, his entire demeanor sort of slumped.

I step in and put my hand on his shoulder. "You okay, Scott?"

"Yes, kiddo, I'm okay."

"My mom looked pretty upset," I say, trying to get him to fill in the gaps.

"We just…said some things that should have been said a long time ago."

I nod, but I don't understand entirely what the big deal is. I assume it's just year after year of having a strange relationship, a forced parenting of sorts over me, but their reactions surprise me.

"Did Nurse Jamie already stop by?" I'm digging for anything that could have set this off.

"All normal, as usual," he says proudly.

I sit on the arm of the chair. "What do you have there?"

He turns the book so I can see the cover, a familiar gray one with a red and pink flower on the front. It's my own copy of *Different Hours*.

"Dunn?" I ask, surprised to see he is reading one of my favorite poets.

"I see why you like him so much."

I smile. "He's witty, funny, and devastatingly dark about

morality. Apparently I'm not the only one who thinks so…"
I nod to the Pulitzer Prize stamp on the cover.

"Just a formality," Scott jokes, the lines on his face attempting to show traces of humor.

"Right…it's the Scott Davis seal of approval that really matters."

He shrugs. "Just make sure you read 'A Postmortem Guide' at my funeral."

"Only if you read it to me now," I insist.

Scott clears his throat. Guilt tugs at me for making him do this.

His eyes are tired, but I can't remember the last time he read to me, and I love the smooth vibrato of his voice when he's lost in the lines of a poem.

I don't focus on the words. I already know it's a beautiful poem, but listening to Scott take on the persona of someone who's already dead and in the ground would be too much to handle.

I stare at his hands, trying to remember if they've changed at all since the first time I saw him grade a paper. I take his in mine, something I never would have done as a teenager but consider a lifeline right now.

They're cold yet clammy, something that both confuses and disturbs me, and I turn to ask him about it. His appearance sends me into a panic.

He's slumped back against the chair, and I have enough wherewithal to hold my hand up to his dry lips. He's breathing, which is a good sign, but I scream for Maddy to call an ambulance because something is wrong with Scott and I have no fucking clue where my phone is.

The world is blurry until I once again find myself

huddled in an ambulance, but this time, Scott is in no state to make demands about the hospital and doctor we head to, so I have to do it. The sirens are deafening, even through the thick metal of the cab, and all I can do is hold his lifeless hand while the paramedics speak in clear tones to one another.

They let me follow them into the hospital, but the nurse insists I have to sit in the waiting room while they take him back. I don't fight her because if I've learned anything from the first time we were here, it's that you do not want to get on a nurse's bad side.

It's only then, in the dreary confines of the waiting room, surrounded by strangers who are drawn together by the fact that we're all waiting for bad news but hoping for good news, that I realize I'm still in my bikini and cover-up. I had enough sense to slip on a pair of my mom's flip-flops, but I have no phone or purse or anything else.

I assumed that Maddy and my mother would follow right behind us, but I don't know for sure.

The teenager across from me recognizes me, but he's busy consoling his mother. I wouldn't even have the patience to indulge a request for a photo right now.

All I can do is cross my arms around my chest and wait in the freezing cold air-conditioning.

I start laughing at myself because I'm being so selfish. Who cares if I'm cold? Scott's lying in a bed alone yet surrounded by strangers, who are poking and prodding at him to bring him back from wherever he has temporarily gone.

At least, I hope it's temporary.

The television drones on and on, and after the fourth

news segment, I wonder where Maddy and my mom are. They aren't as close to Scott as I am, and I know whatever cryfest happened between him and my mom was still fresh, but surely they would want to be here.

Someone sits down next to me, and I breathe in the scent of Noah. I don't have to turn to know it's him, especially when his strong arms pull me into him. I climb into his lap, not caring that it's entirely inappropriate for me to do so, considering what I'm wearing and that we're at his work.

He holds me until my cries have settled down a bit.

"Scott's asking for you," he says.

"He's awake?" I'm surprised by this, but I'm happy because I can't even remember the last thing we said to each other, and words have always been our thing.

"Let's get you a change of clothes first."

Noah leads me to a staff-only area that reminds me of the bathroom and changing rooms I've seen at gyms. He pulls a spare set of scrubs out from his locker and hands them over. I shed my cover-up and pull the pants and shirt over my bathing suit.

"You're cold?" Noah asks but doesn't give me time to answer, just offering me a sweatshirt that I accept gratefully.

"Noah, tell me the truth." I pause, trying to stay strong even though my throat has that awful prickly feeling. "This is the end, isn't it?"

"Yes," Noah says quickly, as if pulling a Band-Aid off.

I can't decide if this helps or hurts.

I follow Noah through the hospital hallways, and I get no warning when we step into Scott's room.

"Took you long enough, kiddo," Scott says. "I've been waiting all day to die, and you've been taking your damn time."

"Scott," I scold as strongly as I can. "You were supposed to make it to New Year's or Halloween or Labor Day or at least the stupid baseball game that's next weekend," I remind him, and my voice breaks.

"Save that crying for later," Scott says. "We need to talk now."

I sniffle. "Okay." I'll do the best I can.

Noah and Scott have some silent conversation over my head, and Noah slips out of the room, closing the door behind him.

"What are you doing with your life?" Scott asks.

"What?" I balk.

He crosses his arms across his chest, trying to appear intimidating, but all I can focus on is the hospital bracelet on his wrist and oxygen monitor on his finger.

"What are *you* doing with *your life*?" he repeats.

"I've been spending the summer—"

"Drowning in my death, not living your life," Scott interrupts. "I'm asking you again. What are you doing with your life?"

"Well, the record label—"

"Is not your life," Scott says sternly, even though his breath is slow, like it hurts him to continue inhaling. "How you make money is not your life. Letting people make decisions for you, floating around cities because you don't have a formidable direction for yourself, running away from your life in California is not your damn life."

I swallow, waiting for him to continue.

"I've been selfish," he continues, glaring at me not to interrupt him. "This time with you has been so wonderful, but at what cost, Liv? I've been dragging you down with me, enabling you to run away from your talent and your whole life just because I'm at the end of mine. It hasn't been fair for you, and now, I'm trying to fix it."

"I don't need you to fix it, Scott," I say quietly. "I just need you to be around for it."

He laughs, and it's hollow and makes him cough. "Well, that's not an option, kiddo. You've got millions of other options, just not that."

I chew on my bottom lip. "I don't want you to die," I croak out as the tears fall.

"Olivia, I'm not going to die," he says.

My heart leaps, but the rational part of me knows that's not possible.

"I'm going to live here." He points to my head, my heart, and finally, my hands. "It's been the highlight of my life to be able to witness and encourage your talent, even for as small of a role I played, and I hope that it sticks with you forever. You have a gift, and it's special, and I know that you've been shunning it, but you've got to let it all in. You need to feel your grief, your frustration, your everything, and know you're capable of transforming it into something beautiful."

I blink, clearing my vision, to take in his resolve.

"Okay," I say because out of all the words in the English language, that's the only one I can say that's not going to cause another wave of tears to fall.

"Okay," Scott returns.

It's the last word he ever says to me.

23

Back when computers were a monstrosity that took up an entire desk with a tower, bulky monitor, large keyboard, and wired mouse, Scott was the only person I knew who had one.

My mother, of course, could never afford one, not that we had a need for it. Maddy was in the same boat, and aside from the brief moments where I could get slow-as-hell internet at the library, Scott's house was the only place I could get online.

Some afternoons after school, I sat in his study, working on my homework and practicing my typing while my mother was at work. I think it was nice for Scott to have someone else at home, and he didn't mind my excitement over looking at the newest videos on YouTube.

Scott's bulky monitor had a built-in webcam and microphone. Looking back, I'm glad that I decided to try my hand at singing instead of joining some of the creepy chat rooms that the girls at school talked about.

I chose a random poem I wrote and tried my best at singing. The video clip was cool, but I wanted to add something extra to it, so I played around with the player-provided editing tools and downloaded some free music clips and distorted the sounds before I mashed it all together.

The rest was history, thanks to a mysterious algorithm that, today, we call virality, which I still don't fully understand.

It's all I can think about during his funeral, one that he had arranged in the solitude of his converted bedroom in my house. It's funny and depressing that our last conversation centered on his encouragement for me to write because when it came time to submit his obituary and write his eulogy, I was completely at a loss.

I pull it together enough to read that fateful Stephen Dunn poem, but that is my only contribution to the day.

I'm stuck on memory lane because it's a distraction from the anger I feel for not being able to write for him. I imagined penning something beautiful and open and soul-crushing, worthy of him and the time we spent together, but I couldn't do it.

When a reporter called, who was definitely more interested in talking to me about me instead of Scott, I passed the phone off to my mother and let her arrange it all.

We have a reception at the funeral home. Noah is by my side, practically holding me up, and I'm vaguely aware of Maddy getting chatted up by Dave, the guy who manages the local grocery and got his heart stomped on by the woman who dyed my hair.

I remember when those trivial things interested me, but now, they feel so distant.

Various people approach me to pay their respects. It's overwhelming, and I'm doing my best, but I'm fading quickly.

To be a writer is to feel everything and channel it into words that people can understand. Scott told me that once, and it's true. I feel it all, every single sympathy and curiosity and feeling of relief that it's not them shrouded in grief.

Finally, I get to go home, but I won't be alone.

I don't know why I insisted so many people live in my house. Maybe I was trying to protect myself from solitude, from falling into the dark spiral that surfaced when Scott's heart stopped beating last week, but I haven't been much for company.

People keep asking me if I'm "okay," and it makes me nauseated.

The day after the funeral, the lawyer calls me, telling me that Scott's will is pretty straightforward. Everything is going to me, except for a few charities that Scott wanted to donate to and some money toward pro bono work at the hospital.

All I want to do is hide from everyone's good intentions, so I do something I've been putting off for a few days since he died—I go back to his house.

I could hire someone to box up all of this stuff, organize it by trash and donation piles, but I feel like at least for this first round of going through his history and belongings, it should be someone who loved him.

Scott wasn't a hoarder, but in some ways, I feel like I

learn even more about him by going through the many boxes of writing and mementos he left behind. His poetry is pure gold, and I can't wait to sift through it all. I stick those in a small box I'm using to take back home with me.

I take over the floor of his living room and organize a stack of photos. I should have these digitized and kept safe from fingerprints, but I can't help but flip through them now. I find a few school pictures of myself over the years, but I focus my efforts on continuing my journey backward into his life.

There are a ton of photos of Beth, and a few of them together, but it's one picture, buried at the bottom of the pile, that makes me want to faint.

Had she not looked so much like me when she was younger, that mousy brown hair, the same nose, I would have passed right by it. It's my mother, staring at the camera amid a fit of laughter, a man beside her.

The picture was taken long before selfies were popular, so I can only assume that the camera was propped up somehow and both of the people in the photograph dashed in the frame before the timer hit.

If it was just a photograph of my mother, I would be confused but come up with some plausible explanation, but I recognize that man who has his hands around her waist the same exact way it's wrapped around Beth's in others.

Scott and my mother...something happened between them.

I break out into a cold sweat and barrel out of his house, but it seems I can't get home fast enough. I swear I hit every goddamn red light.

My mother is unassuming, sitting on the couch and flipping through a magazine, her last moment of peace before I explode over the past.

"What the actual fuck is this?" I demand.

She's startled, and I don't give her time to recover. I shove the photograph in her face with shaking hands. Her face falls.

I'm absolutely livid that she is taking her time telling me the truth, so I yell at her again. "Explain!" I don't know how to get this anger outside of my body any other way than yelling.

She presses a hand to her mouth, and she looks like she's about to cry. I'm losing patience rapidly.

"It's...I can explain," she says quietly. "If you'll just sit down and hear me out."

"What other fucking choice do I have? It's not like I can ask Scott."

I'm so mad that those words aren't even painful to say.

They had a secret, and I'm shaking at the possibility that he could be...more than my high school English teacher and writing mentor.

She gestures for the seat beside her on the couch, but I collapse in the armchair.

She swallows and tries to compose herself. "Your father and I—"

"Is Scott my father?" I ask, needing this question answered more than everything else.

"No," she says quickly. "I'll admit everything would have been...better if he was."

I grind my teeth, mentally willing her to hurry the fuck up.

"Scott, your father, and I were best friends. We grew

up in the same neighborhood and always seemed to have identical schedules at school, and we did everything together." She pauses. "Well, until your father and I started dating, and he…transformed into someone else. Your father had a temper, but he became more territorial and jealous and accusatory, putting up walls between us and our social group. At the time, I thought it was love…"

My anger dissipates into something helpless.

"Scott saw the bruises and tried to help. It was a mess, to say the least, especially when Scott and I realized that our feelings for each other went beyond friendship. But I was scared, Liv. So scared and vulnerable, and when I found out I was pregnant…"

She stops, as if the words are too painful to say out loud.

"When you found out you were pregnant," I prompt.

"Scott was the first one I told. I was completely panicked about what to do. I was so young, so stuck in this town, and I…" She stops, looking at me with guilt in her eyes. "Fast forward a few months, Scott and your father had a big blowup. Your father left town, but still after everything, I was furious. Because Scott was leaving for college, and without your father, I felt so damn alone."

I knew my grandparents wanted nothing to do with my mom's teenage pregnancy, but I never heard the other parts of this story in so much detail before.

"What did you do?" I ask.

"Stayed with friends after I told Scott off," she answers. "Your father eventually came back, for a little while, but he took off again pretty soon after that. Truly, I don't know where he is now, but I wouldn't be surprised if he over-dosed or drank himself to death a long time ago."

"So that's why your relationship with Scott has been so strained all this time," I say, almost laughing at the real-ization.

"By the time I got my life together, got us situated and got through beauty school...he and Beth were engaged." She laughs. "I wanted to throw up every single time I saw them together."

I frown, but she leans over to squeeze my hand.

"It was nice having him here though," she says. "It was a good way to clear the air and...say goodbye."

I clutch the picture in between my fingertips as I try to take in all this new information.

My mom leaves me alone at some point, giving me some time to process.

It's funny how mad I was at the start of this conversa-tion, considering how much I ache for everything my mother went through as a teenager.

It bothers me how much I relate to her in this moment. Granted, we had completely different sets of events happen to us in our teenage years, but like me, so much was out of her control during that time, and that feeling stuck with us.

If my father and Scott hadn't stepped in, what would my mother be doing now? Would she be here, working part-time at the nail salon, spending most of her days alone in a giant house? What would I be doing without Noah? Had he left me to my own devices, would I be this some-what successful failure?

Why did it work out for me and not for her?

That's the most heartbreaking part of all of this. That

my mother, who I harbored resentment for during most of my life, was helpless, and I was ungrateful for the sacrifices she made for me.

An apology wouldn't be enough.

I couldn't tell her I was sorry and have it make up for all the little petty thoughts in my mind over the years, how resentful I was of her for how she lived her life, how she acted around others.

I remember what Scott told me the day he died, about how I needed to start living my own life, really living and not just going along with whatever someone else had decided for me.

Because of me, my mother didn't get a chance to discover or chase after her dream, and because of laziness or selfishness or disinterest, I was letting mine crumble to dust.

The only way forward was to return to LA, to make my own decisions and to move forward. I'm not running away just for the sake of doing so. In fact, I'm not running away at all, but the thought of leaving Maddy, Liam, my mother, and Noah, most of all, makes me want to stay put.

For once in my life, though, I need to face everything head on.

I grab my keys and decide to do the hardest one first.

My resolve wavers as I drive over to Noah's house, but I try to hold strong. I need to tell him everything that I've learned from my mother, to make him understand everything that I'm feeling, and to temporarily say goodbye.

I'm not sure how long I'll be gone, but I know that a long-distance relationship isn't an option for us. I barely manage to see him when we live a short drive away, let alone a five-hour flight, and frankly, I need time to myself, to truly be on my own, with no record label scheduling out my life or manager to run things for me.

But when Noah opens the door, I can't help but launch myself at him. Words aren't exchanged between us. We just move together.

Our clothes are flung off as we fall into his bed, and I stare at the ceiling while he moves over me. He whispers promises against my skin. It's only been a week since we last did this, and I've missed it so much.

I don't know how I will keep it together once I'm gone, but that's exactly what I will need to figure out.

Noah's lips capture mine, and I need to get out of my own head, to focus on this moment between us. I push him backward and right myself on top of him. We both cry out when I sink down and he's inside of me, even more when I start moving.

Up and down.

Up and down.

Up and down.

His fingertips dig into my hips, and I hold onto his neck so that I can catch his mouth as we find our release. Me first, then him.

In the seconds after it happens, I collapse on top of him. He pulls me against him. I wince when he slides himself out of me, but being in his arms is pure bliss.

We lay together.

He plays with my hair, and I try to listen to the sound of his heart beating in his chest. "Where are you right now?" Noah asks.

I blink. Either I'm more transparent or Noah is more

attuned to me than I thought. Both options don't exactly invoke feelings of comfort.

I'm trying my best to be here, in the moment with him, but I feel a pull elsewhere.

"Miles and miles away," I admit.

He rolls over on his side, and his lips are soft against my neck. "Come back."

We repeat the motions again, but this time, it's slower, more appreciative.

It's a sweet goodbye.

He just doesn't know it yet.

Later, when we curl up semi-clothed on his couch after a dinner of raiding whatever was in his pantry, he finally faces me.

"Why do I get the feeling when I wake up tomorrow morning, you're going to be gone?"

I smile sadly. "Because it's true."

I already booked my flight and packed a small bag of my toiletries, electronics, and Scott's journals and favorite books.

He stops touching me immediately, leaning forward with his elbows on his knees and his gaze on the floor. "Were you even going to tell me?"

"Yes," I say. "Of course."

"Look, Olivia, I know you're upset about Scott—"

"This isn't about Scott. This is about me." I stand because I need to say these things to him so that he'll hear me, and I don't know if I am strong enough yet to resist the pull to curl up into him and never come back out.

"My life is temporary, Noah. Or at least, it has been. Going from one concert venue, one house, one city over and over again on repeat. I need to figure out how to make things permanent, how to be on my own, and how to decide what I really want."

Noah's gaze meets mine. I see all of the warmth he has for me in his eyes, but I also know that he is fixing a calm, cool mask of indifference on his face.

It's self-preservation, and it's what I saw for four years in the halls of Hill High School.

"So you're just going to leave? Run away from all your problems and reality?"

"Excuse me?"

"You left when things were hard, Olivia, I get it," Noah says. "You needed to do it, but we're not goddamn teenagers anymore, and you can't just run away from your problems."

I put my hands on my hips. "This is why I need to leave, Noah. I'm doing the exact opposite of running."

"You're afraid, and this is an excuse. You're devastated about Scott, trust me, I understand, but you need to stay here and deal with this."

"What I need is for you not to lecture me on what I need and what I think," I fire back.

"So, you're really just going to pack up and go then?"

He's angry, and I take one more chance at honesty with him. "I just have this feeling that this block inside, this revolt against my creativity and my ability to write, it's buried in me somewhere that I need to reconnect with."

"Well, I certainly hope this gives you something to fucking write about," Noah says, voice full of venom.

In this moment, he's not the supportive, selfless Noah he has been, he's the bully who wants to gut me, to make fun of the knock-off designer bag my mom got me for Christmas.

I stare at him, watching the hard shell overtake him. I close my eyes, wishing that I found a better way to end this, but I should have known it wouldn't be easy.

When I look at him one final time, a tear of betrayal cuts down my cheek, and the movement of it rights Noah, as if he realized he made a big mistake.

I don't give him a chance to correct it.

I'm out the door, in my car, and holding back tears so that I can make the drive home in one piece.

Thankfully, the two and a half people who live in my house are nowhere to be found, even though it's just after dinner time on a weeknight. Before I went to Noah's, I bought a one-way ticket for the first flight out tomorrow morning, but that seems too long to wait now.

I pull up an app on my phone, and I'm pleased that there's a red-eye flight. I have enough time to call a car service, the same one we used to go to the theatre downtown, so I shower, collect myself, and head to the airport to make the flight.

After I board, I shoot my mom and Maddy texts, letting them know I had something urgent to take care of in LA and that I'd text them when I land.

Had it been just two months since I last sat in a cushy airplane seat?

Back then, I was nervous as hell, late, and already counting down the days until I could return. Now, I'm taking off into the unknown, and it's strange how comforting it feels.

24

FIVE MONTHS LATER

It's New Year's Eve.

I haven't stopped thinking about Scott since the moment I woke up this morning in the unfamiliar surroundings of a tiny New York City hotel room.

I barely got this gig, and it was the only one I've ever really pushed for in my career. I knew one of the organizers from my performance last year, which gave me an in, but it wasn't until I sent a recording of what I planned to sing that they agreed to it.

Performances before the ball drops are a little weird because we're past Christmas, so those peppy songs are no longer appropriate, but it's too early to figure out how to set the tone for the new year.

It's frigid outside now that the sun has officially set, and I'm at my place on the stage, just waiting for the cue from the person behind the camera. This song is a big leap from my past work, but somehow, it's rooted in it, evolving just as I have.

I get the countdown from the producer, and I'm officially live, broadcasting to millions of screens.

I expect the magical feeling of performing to overtake me, but it doesn't. I don't find another plane of existence among the random falling confetti and crowd noise; I just feel the cold.

Trying to push past it, I start on the piano, but my hands are too frozen to perform. I suffered through months of piano lessons for this moment, and it turns out, it was for nothing.

Scott would be proud of me for learning and trying, but it doesn't feel right.

I'm not supposed to be frozen and jittery for this moment—I'm supposed to feel easy warmth pulsating through my body as I bring my poetry to life through music.

I stop my attempt and have to scramble on how to recover. As if this massive audience isn't enough to falter in front of, I already know this performance is going to make its way to YouTube immediately after. I don't want to give any negative fodder.

The best I can hope for is to start a cappella and pray that one of the people behind the camera can figure a way to weave in the music from the file I sent originally, but I'm not going to depend on that—I'm just going to do what I can.

I'm vaguely aware of the panic around me, but I move away from the piano, a beautiful, white grand at that, and grab the mic.

When I open my mouth, I'm not in front of an audience or cameras and lights and television workers. I'm the introverted sixteen-year-old girl who sat in a hallway after school, writing poetry, excited to play with the weird sounds on the computer that I could barely use.

The first line comes out, and I'm thinking about the first time Scott read my work, the moment I read it aloud to the class and incited Noah's anger. Scott was so well-intentioned and enthusiastic, and I wonder how different things would have been if my mother followed him to college or he stayed behind.

I certainly wouldn't be standing here.

Noah mocked me in the hallway after that class, reciting the lines he remembered. The tears poured down my face then and now as I pick up the chorus and the words soar. All of my emotion falls into the song, and it takes over my entire body.

I can't help pouring my entire soul into the words I'm singing.

> *[Verse 1]*
> *Past versions of*
> *Nightmares dislodged by daydreams*
> *Ourselves and what reality they live in*
> *Expectations unmet*
>
> *It was dark and bitter and us*
> *Clouded by unseen transformations*
> *That taste like summer and potential*
> *In the present*
>
> *[Chorus]*
> *Do you want to live here,*

with me,
in the now?

[Verse 2]
For all the promises and eulogies,
The things that I should have said

Press it all back
Down into the past
We don't need it
Nobody does

[Chorus]
Do you want to live here,
with me,
in the now?

[Bridge]
There's something about this state
That feels so evergreen
And I want to breathe it in

[Chorus]
Do you want to live here,
with me,
in the now?

As I drop the final note, I take a deep breath. The tears fall, dotting the front of my jeweled dress, and I look around. The group of people around me are all speechless, and there's a beat until they break out in applause.

Performing again, after all these months, feels almost as good as it did on that open mic night.

Only then, I had Noah waiting for me. Now, I have an empty hotel room with a warm bottle of champagne sitting on the dresser.

"And that was Olivia O, performing her new, independently produced single 'In The Now.'"

Everyone congratulates me as I walk off stage, but I don't feel elated. It wasn't the performance I envisioned, and I'm too caught up in my emotions to relax. I'm glad I don't have to do an interview because, frankly, I said everything I wanted to say in those lyrics.

Adam, of course, attacks me when I am back in the makeshift green room.

"Oh my fucking goodness, O, that was…something else," he says, nearly in hysterics.

One of his artists performed a few acts before me, and he stayed around as a friend to support me, even though I didn't ask him to. I suppose the open bar and cute bartender didn't hurt anything.

"Thank you," I say politely. "And I appreciate you staying behind for moral support."

"I almost regretted it when you stopped playing the piano. I could have had a heart attack, but you pulled it off. You know, I bet if I talked to the bosses at my company, they'd let me bring you—"

I shake my head.

He rolls his eyes. "Of course, these big plans you have but won't clue me in on."

"Soon enough," I promise, hugging him goodbye.

I cling to my winter jacket like it's a life raft. With a

scarf wrapped around my neck and my hood up, no one gives me a second glance.

Once I'm out of Times Square, thanks to a secret pathway that only performers know about, I head back to the hotel. It's only a few blocks away, but I need the chilly New York air more than anything else right now. I hear the screams of the countdown to midnight, and when the ball drops, I'm standing alone on the sidewalk.

Loneliness has been my friend since I left Pittsburgh.

Writers love solitude because it lets them feel their emotions as big or as small as they want to and then do what they want with it.

For me, it meant taking a Sharpie to the pristine white walls of my condo, letting my brain and hand do their thing without second-guessing. It was amazing for my productivity, and somewhere between the pages of Scott's writing and my own mind, my creativity came back.

In a moment of anger, Noah insinuated that I could use the emotions tied up in us to further my career. He meant it as a slight, but it was actually true. I didn't feel much when I got divorced, got dropped by my label, or got roasted online, but I did feel every single thing in the weeks we spent together.

Months have passed since then, but my feelings remain the same.

I miss those lazy summer days at the pool with Maddy and Liam just as much as I miss those evenings with Noah.

My mother actually came out to see me in LA for Thanksgiving, and Maddy and I talk on the phone a few times a week. I'd asked her to help clear out Scott's house while I was gone, now that I had the only things I wanted to keep in my possession. She refused payment for the work, even when it started eating up her free time outside her new job in hospital administration.

On Christmas Day, she unwrapped the deed to his house, which I transferred into her name.

As much as I wished they could have been here with me, it was the final thing I wanted to do on my own, the end of my healing process.

In it, I found the answer to the question I never asked myself—the question Scott asked me.

What are you doing with your life?

"I'm going to start my own record label with a publishing arm. I'm going to find teenage voices that need amplification, and I'm going to help them the best I can, whether it be through music or written words. I'm going to get out of my own head, my own selfishness, and help other people in any way I can, like Scott helped me."

I say the words into the night sky, and the smile stays on my face as light snowflakes fall against my skin.

By the time I step off the elevator and head toward my room, I'm exhausted and ready for a good night's sleep.

Aside from final preparations for the show, I've spent the last week packing up my small life in Los Angeles with the intent to move back to my house in Pennsylvania. I can work from anywhere, catch a flight whenever I need to, but being away from Maddy, Liam, and my mom...that's non-negotiable.

I'm shrugging off my boots and outerwear when there's a knock at my door.

It's almost one in the morning, and I assume it's

someone trying to enter the wrong room. I ignore it until the rapping on the door hits again.

I sigh and close one eye to stare into the peephole.

"It's me," Noah says.

I gasp and slide the chain and unlock the deadbolt so that I can see him with my own eyes.

"How?" I ask.

"Airplane, yesterday afternoon," Noah says as light-heartedness and seriousness fight for ownership of his features.

"Oh," I say, waving him in.

My room is a mess, and so am I.

I hadn't expected to see him, obviously, and I'm on the brink of a freakout. I hadn't come up with a plan on how to get Noah back yet, even if he still wanted me, but his presence here is clear, and it's all I can do to not fling myself at him.

Noah sits down at the edge of the bed and looks up at me. He's just as handsome as he was the last time I saw him, of course, and my body immediately aches for him.

He reaches for my hands, and I don't hesitate to hold his in my own.

"I know you wanted Scott to be here for you on New Year's Eve," Noah says slowly. "I was wondering if you would let me be here instead."

The thoughtfulness of the gesture moves me, and I kiss him with everything I've been holding back these past few months.

It's familiar and lovely. I'm ready to get lost in him, to pick up where we left off, but first, I need clarification on this whole *thing* with Noah *fucking* Washington.

I pull back and laugh at the groan that escapes his lips. "Did you hear my performance?" I ask him.

"Hear it? I lived it."

"Well, are you going to answer the question, Noah Washington?" I ask him.

"Let's do it," he says. "Let's live in the now for the rest of our lives."

There's a drop of a knee, an emerald ring, a kiss of agreement, and many other promises made.

ACKNOWLEDGMENTS

I am forever grateful to the book blogging community for the endless support and excitement over my work. The reviews, pictures, and general love has felt like the biggest bear hug through my computer screen, and I'm so grateful to have met so many awesome people online who love to read as much as I do.

I need to thank Taylor Starek, as always, for being such a wonderful editor and ruthless red-liner. I'm so grateful for your direction, reassurance, and changes to make my stories so much stronger.

Lindsay Hallowell has saved me from making horrific grammar and punctuation mistakes on numerous occasions, and I'm so grateful to have your eyes, brain, and support on my work. Plus, selfishly, I've learned so much from you!

My family and friends, you all are wonderful humans who have listened to me ramble about people, places, and drama that doesn't exist anywhere but my own head. Thank you so much for your reassurance and support.

And, finally, to my readers. Thank you for taking a chance on this book—my first foray into new adult fiction has been a lot of fun, and I hope you enjoyed my step out of the young adult world. (I, personally, love being able to swear so much—well, just a bit more than usual.)

ABOUT THE AUTHOR

Jennifer Ann Shore is a writer and an Amazon bestselling author based in Seattle, Washington.

She has written multiple fiction novels, including "New Wave," a young adult dystopian, and "The Extended Summer of Anna and Jeremy," a young adult romance.

In her decade of working in journalism, marketing, and book publishing, she has won numerous awards for her work from companies such as Hearst and SIIA.

Be sure to visit her website (https://www.jenniferannshore.com) and follow her on Twitter (@JenniferAShore), Instagram (@shorely), or your preferred social media channel to stay in touch.